Familiar

Spirits

DON'T READ BEFORE BEDTIME!

Familiar
Spirits

Compiled by
Donald J. Bingle &
William Pack

Edited by
Donald J. Bingle

This book is published by
54°40' Orphyte, Inc.
St. Charles, Illinois

**54°40'
ORPHYTE,
INC.**

ISBN 13: 978-0692532959
ISBN: 0692532951

October 2015

Beware! Take care!
Close eyes; pull covers tight.
For ghosts and spirits dare
walk through these pages tonight.

Table of Contents

Introduction

WHAT KINDS of ghost stories do you remember? What deathly tales do you retell? What horrible manifestations do you wish you could forget?

Ghost stories frighten us because deep down everyone believes in ghosts. Every culture tells tales of departed spirits roaming the earth. Many of us have had personal encounters which still haunt us, whether during the dead of night or the flickering shadows of waking day. So we whistle past graveyards, sleep with the nightlight on, and hide under the covers when we hear noises we can't rationally explain.

Worse yet, we believe ghosts can harm us in body, mind, and spirit. We believe they are evil and can rip us asunder, force us to commit unspeakable acts, or consume our souls.

We try to dismiss ghosts as the stuff of superstition and folklore, but we all secretly want to know if our ghostly beliefs are true, if our reality is a lie. We yearn for proof, yet tremble at the prospect of having our beliefs confirmed. We quiver and quake not only because we fear what may happen to us while we live, but because we fear what may happen to us, what may become of us, when we die.

I admit, I am not a fan of the various ghost-hunting and paranormal investigation "reality" shows on television. A flicker of shadow or a random noise in a decaying building is hardly credible evidence of anything, much less conclusive proof of inter-dimensional life after death. Besides, ghosts who can spike an E.M.F. (electro-magnetic frequency) detector or mumble indistinctly in captured E.V.P. (electronic voice phenomena) are hardly the stuff of legend.

Ghosts who haunt and harm, ghosts who deceive and destroy, ghosts who are on a quest—for evil or for redemption—those are the sinister spirits which frighten and interest me. Their tales are the types of dark and unsettling ghost stories which have been gathered in this collection of *Familiar Spirits*.

Some of the authors of this anthology have confessed to me their stories are based on personal experience; others have maintained a discreet silence. But whether the ghosts in the stories that follow seek solace, sympathy, closure, company, vengeance, or fresh victims, they all want something.

They will not be denied.

So, gentle reader, find a comfortable corner where you feel safe and turn the pages of *Familiar Spirits* in horror and fascination until you are too disturbed to continue. After all, reading is a journey into other worlds which you always take alone.

Visit these darkened realms, then try to sleep and see what haunts you in the deep recesses of forgotten memory.

Donald J. Bingle
August 2015

The Cold Earth
Sarah Hans

MY HUSBAND, Tom, killed me on the first of May, angry because I overcooked the meatloaf. It was the last straw for both of us. When he grabbed my hair and slammed my head against the kitchen counter, I thought about how I had known for years this would be my inevitable end.

Nobody survives living with a psychopath.

Tom buried me in the backyard beneath the old oak tree, where we'd shared our first kiss when I was only a blushing girl of seventeen. Even in death, I could still feel his hot breath on my face, his hands skimming my supple young body, the urgency of his erection pressed against my hip, as if it were happening at that very moment. I called out to the younger me, tried to warn her, but she just went right on kissing him.

My grave was cold beneath the oak, under the earth. My flesh melted away and my meat was eaten by worms. The tree's roots tickled my bones, wrapping around me in a woody embrace.

Mama never liked Tom. She wouldn't let us marry, so we eloped against her wishes the day I turned eighteen. Mama refused to speak to me after that. She was never a nice woman, not generous with a smile or a hug or even a kind word, but now I think maybe she did try to protect me, in the end.

Maybe she did love me.

She died about a year after we eloped, killed by her two-pack-a-day habit, so we moved into the old farmhouse. It was convenient since Tom had lost his job and we were about to be evicted. He wouldn't let me work to help make ends meet. He said no wife of his would hold a job, like the concept was dirty and repulsive. I thought that was romantic, I thought he wanted to provide for me and take care of me. Wasn't that sweet? I didn't see that he was trying to control me. I didn't understand that he was cutting me off from the rest of the world and keeping me dependent on him. I didn't realize until things got bad.

Without a job, Tom turned to a life of crime. At first, he told me he was working third shift at the sandpaper factory in town. One day at the grocery store, one of the few places I was allowed to go alone, I overheard two women talking about how hard the factory closing was on their families. I confronted Tom about the lie and he hit me for the first time. Just once, on the face, just a slap, but hard enough to leave a handprint for a few days.

I packed my things and went to a friend's place. Tom came after me. He apologized. He brought me flowers. He told me he'd never hit me again. He promised things would be different, better. I was naive and silly and went back to him.

And things were better, for a while. But soon he was bringing suspicious packages home, hiding stolen cars in the barn, filing the serial numbers off firearms in the living room. My protests fell on deaf ears. He kept the only set of car keys. He canceled the phone service. My once-a-week visits to the grocery store were my only opportunity to see other people, and those were closely guarded. I became a prisoner.

I tried walking to town, once, and got picked up by a couple of Tom's "colleagues" halfway there. They took me home. Tom locked me in the root cellar for two days in punishment and then made me burn all my shoes.

I never tried to run away again.

Those days were full of so much turmoil, so many hot tears, so much fear, so much hatred. Now, below the ground, it's cool and dry and my fear is replaced by the wisdom of the earth, the songs of trees, the whispered secrets of twining roots and digging beetles. Up above, the living scurry and rush, but down here we grow and decay and wait.

I am the worms that devour my flesh, the roots that coil about my bones. I am the cool night breeze and the warm summer soil. I am forgotten and at peace.

But then I hear a voice. A woman's voice. Laughing. I am her, and she is me, flirting with Tom beneath the oak tree. He murmurs something, he smiles. He stands on my grave and seduces her with promises. *I have money, baby girl, I have a whole house.* He can protect her, he can care for her. She's as young as I was when we first met, slim as a willow, breasts like mosquito bites and hip bones jutting into his hands as he touches her, persuading her with caresses and kisses. He's kind and attentive and charming, oh so charming, with that white smile and those blue, blue eyes.

My heart hurts, even though it was devoured by worms months ago. Emotions rush into the empty space that once was me. I have no throat to scream my pain, no lips to make words, but it's too much. I can't watch him do this all over again. The earth groans, the oak tree sways, and a branch tears away from the trunk without warning, crashing to the ground below. Tom dances out of the way and the branch narrowly misses the girl, who squeaks in alarm.

They laugh in relief and he puts his arm about her possessively, protectively, pulling her toward the house. He turns and looks back at the tree as they mount the porch and I see a flicker of recognition in his eyes.

Fear races through me, stinging like that first slap to my cheek. He knows I'm down here. He knows that branch was sent for him. I shrink back into the cool embrace of my grave, trying to will myself into nonexistence. I am dirt and worms and roots now. I am nothing. If I forget myself, then maybe he'll forget me, too.

Days and weeks pass in the darkness beneath the oak tree. Tom forgets about the branch, forgets about me again. The girl moves into the farmhouse with him. I don't want to hear their voices, but I do; even through six feet of soil, I can hear them laughing, making plans, making love. If I had ears, I'd pack them full of dirt, but I don't, so there's no way to block the two of them out. I draw the tree's roots tighter around my skeleton, sinking deeper into the earth, trying to find an end for this nightmare.

Winter comes, and I get some respite. The voices are muffled now that Tom and his new bride spend most of their time indoors and the plants that serve as my eyes and ears doze in hibernation.

I hear my name, *Megan*, and the sound rouses me from

6

slumber. Tom's friends have gathered around a bonfire in the yard, not far from my resting place. *Jessica's a real pretty girl. Don't know how you keep getting women that good looking, Tommy. That Megan was a fine piece of ass, too. Whatever happened to her?*

None of your damn business.

Rage courses through me, cold as ice and hot as a brand. The oak's roots lash beneath me in response. I seek the heat of the fire, pushing at the earth. The men shout as the bonfire bursts apart, embers flying and burning logs rolling out of the fire ring. Someone shrieks, and I can smell the gut-churning stench of searing human flesh. The others tackle him with a blanket and put out the flames. He groans. *My leg, my leg!*

Christ, his jeans are melted to his skin. Someone call 9-1-1!

No! What're you thinking? We got a barn full of hot cars. Drive him to the hospital your damn selves.

They trundle the injured man into a car. I hear the sounds of many car doors slamming, engines revving, and then a fleet of cars and motorcycles drives off the property. Left behind, Tom curses and shouts, kicking at the smoldering logs and abandoned beer bottles. Jessica tries to calm him, telling him it'll be okay. She convinces him to go back inside and get some sleep.

The cold, blissful silence of winter snaps back into place the next morning and stays that way for another month. Then, the ground thaws. Rain falls instead of snow. Seeds begin to germinate, pushing new life into the soil. Wriggling worms breed in my eye sockets and fresh roots visit my earthy hideaway, humming the cheerful songs of green things growing.

Jessica decides to take up gardening, so Tom brings her seeds and flowers. She kneels in the yard, pulling weeds and hoeing the earth, dropping in seeds and patting the soil over them. She's very tender, very sweet, singing Guns 'n Roses love ballads to the sprouting plants and walking barefoot through the grass.

She and Tom get in a fight one night when he pours a bottle of beer over her garden. He locks her out of the house. She curls up on the porch, sobbing, one hand over her throbbing jaw. I remember the sharp pain of a fresh bruise as it blossomed purple across my face. She is me and I am her. She is too tender, too kind, too young for this. It took Tom several years to be this cruel to me, and they've been married for barely one. He'll kill her soon, like he did me, without even meaning to do it. And then her body will join mine, and we'll be together, sisters in death, the roots pressing us into a cool, final caress of bone on bone.

I'm lonely, but not lonely enough to watch Tom murder again.

I can save the girl yet.

The trees sway and rattle. The flowers tremble and whisper. Jessica sits up and looks at her garden.

Jessssssiiiiiiicaaaaaaaaa.

She scrambles to her feet and runs to the door, pounding on it with her fists, shrieking and wailing. Floorboards creak as Tom moves through the house. The door opens and his fist thrusts out, catching her on the cheek, sending her tumbling back to the porch.

Please, Tommy, please don't leave me out here. It's haunted!

He pauses in the open door. *What'd you say?*

She sobs, hysterical, clutching at the porch railing as if it's a lifeline. *There's a ghost. It called my name.*

Tom strides out of the house, across the porch, to the barn. He returns with two shovels, presenting one to Jessica. He leads her to the oak tree and gestures to the place where he buried me. *Dig,* he says.

I should feel afraid. He's coming for me, again, one final time. But as they move the rain-softened soil away from my bones, I welcome them. What can he do to me in death, after all, that is worse than what he did to me in life? The earth is my flesh now, every tree and bush and blade of grass an extension of my ghostly body. I have power in death I did not possess in life.

Are ... are those bones?

Keep digging. We need to get the whole skeleton.

Who is this, Tommy? Who did you bury? Is it Megan? Did you kill her?

Stop asking questions and dig, girl, if you don't want to hear no more ghost voices.

No. I won't keep going unless you tell me what happened. Who is this?

Tom raises his fist and lunges toward Jessica. My rage rushes up the oak tree and snaps another of its branches. The branch falls between them, hitting Tom's upraised arm. He bellows in pain.

Jessica scrambles for the edge of the hole while Tom is distracted. The soil is slippery and she's panicking, unable to gain purchase. I command the roots that are my fingers to

9

make a ladder for her. She gasps for a moment, unable to comprehend what she's seeing as the roots intertwine before her very eyes.

Growling, Tom reaches for her again. She squeaks and scales the ladder, kicking away Tom's groping fingers. Tom tries to follow her up the ladder, but the roots retract as soon as Jessica is safe. He slides down the side of the hole and collapses, flailing, onto my skeleton.

The tree branches scratch and scrape together to make the sound of my terrible laughter.

I command the roots to lift me. My corpse slides from beneath Tom, rising up in the air high above him, above the hole in the earth. The moon bathes me in her silvery glow, illuminating my clean-picked bones wrapped in roots, coiled with worms, dropping beetles from above. My grin is white and menacing. The tarp in which Tom buried me trails behind me like a dark veil, fluttering and snapping in the breeze.

Until death do us part, the grasses whisper.

Jessica screams. Tom curses my name. The roots which are my arms reach up and close around him, pulling him down into the cool embrace of the grave.

Jessica plants hyacinths over my grave so I can enjoy their sweet perfume every spring. She visits the oak often to sit beneath its creaking branches. She talks to me, telling me about the life growing in her belly, the postman she's going to marry, and the family she plans to have so she can fill the farmhouse with laughter and love as it should be.

She teaches her children to swing on a tire hung from the

oak's branches. The children dig holes in the earth to whisper their secrets and longings to the oak's roots. I cradle them in my branches and protect them from sudden storms beneath my canopy.

When Jessica's eldest daughter is sixteen, a boy driving a Mustang arrives to take her on a date. Jessica walks out to the oak tree to lean against my trunk, pressing her forehead to my rough exterior as she has so many times before.

She wipes tears from her cheeks. *I don't like this boy, Mother Megan. He reminds me of Tommy.*

Tom writhes and gurgles at the sound of his name, but the oak's roots coil more tightly about him, like a constrictor squeezing her prey, until he silences.

I don't like the boy either.

All I've Got is a Photograph
Dolores Whitt Becker

"I DREAMED about Mari." I didn't realize I had spoken aloud until Dennis curled around me and nuzzled.

"Is that a good thing?" His voice was blurry with sleep.

"Of course it's a good thing." I rolled over and faced him. "How could it not be?"

"Could be upsetting, is all."

"I s'pose. But it'd still be a good thing, too, I think. I've been … hoping for it." I'd almost said 'praying,' but Dennis was a devout atheist and I'd learned to avoid such words unless I wanted a gently earnest dissertation. I was agnostic myself and the thought of using the word felt odd, anyway. Appealing to some cosmic benefactor for favors seemed like cheating if I didn't acknowledge said Being for any other reason. If I'd been calling out to any spiritual entity, it would more likely have been Mari herself, asking her to visit my dreams, although even that was pushing the boundaries of my personal cosmology. I didn't believe in the continuation of the soul, or what have you, after death. At least, I'd been pretty certain about that for some time before Mari died.

It seemed dishonest to reverse direction on something like that once I had a personal stake in it. Yet, I could almost feel her lingering presence.

"It was just a dream," I muttered, irritated with myself now. "I've forgotten most of it already."

"Do you dream about him, too?" Dennis asked over breakfast, nodding toward the only picture we had up that included my ex-husband. It was a shopping mall studio portrait we'd had taken when Mari was a toddler, back when we'd been a genuinely happy little family. It seemed like another lifetime.

"Geoff?" I shrugged, bothered by the question more than I wanted to let on. "Maybe. I hardly ever remember my dreams. This probably wasn't the first time I've dreamed about Mari."

"So you don't remember any dreams about him."

"Not really, no. Why do you care? You can't be jealous; he's dead. And I didn't love him any more by that time, anyway. Even if he was still alive, you wouldn't have anything to worry about."

"I'm not worried about that."

"So what are you worried about?"

"Who says I'm worried about anything? I just asked a question. Jesus." Dennis got up and went to brush his teeth.

What was that about? Maybe 'worried' wasn't the right word, but there was more than idle curiosity in Dennis' question. Something was eating at him.

I had a little time after he left for work before I had to leave as well. As I tidied up the breakfast things, I felt restless, almost twitchy, to the point that I nearly dropped a dish more than once. *Fretful*, that was what it was, as if something was gnawing at the back of my brain. I almost felt that someone was watching me. My eyes returned again and again to the photograph of Geoff, Mari, and me, smiling out at the world, blissfully unaware of what the future held for us.

Except that Geoff wasn't smiling. I looked away, shut my eyes, took a deep breath and summoned my memory of the picture. I had looked at it thousands of times in the years since it had been taken; I knew exactly what the expressions on our faces were. All three of us were smiling.

Until now. When I opened my eyes, Geoff was still staring straight out at me. His expression had gone from cheerful to neutral, almost hostile.

"No stinking way," I muttered and turned my back on the portrait.

I fumbled through my day, glad to be away from it, but also impatient to get home and look again, arguing with myself over whether I had really seen what I thought I'd seen. How could it be possible?

When I got home, the picture was just as it had always been, but I couldn't shake the image of what I'd seen after breakfast. I grabbed a bottle of wine and a glass and went into the living room. I remembered the brooding look on Geoff's face not only from earlier that morning, but from countless 'discussions' about our disintegrating marriage.

When Dennis got home, I was halfway through my third leisurely glass and hadn't even thought about dinner, much less prepared anything. I hadn't thought about much of anything; mostly, I'd been trying not to think about a lot of things. Dennis was quiet. He said more to the guy taking his phone order at the Chinese take-out than he did to me. We ate our

Mongolian beef and pot stickers in silence.

"Okay, maybe I am worried," he said as we got ready for bed.

"Why?" I asked, when he didn't go on right away. I wasn't entirely sober yet, but I was close enough to it to trust myself to have a reasonable conversation.

"I guess … I wonder if you've grieved sufficiently. For him, I mean," Dennis continued quickly. "I know you're still grieving for Mari, but it seems like you've just closed the lid on him."

"It's not the same," I replied quietly. 'It's not the same, at all."

"Okay, granted. But still … you can want the guy out of your life and still be sorry that he's dead."

"I am sorry that he's dead. It was a tragic waste of human potential. But you have to understand two things … I had no emotional investment in him, by that time. That was what I had to do, for my own good. And, he did it to himself."

"I know all that. I still wonder. I can't help thinking it should take longer to get him out of your system."

"I got most of him out of my system before he died. And I did mourn his death, but I didn't linger over it. And I don't want to talk about it anymore. At least, not tonight." I got into bed. Still fuzzy from the wine, I decided to forego my usual half hour or so of reading and go straight to sleep.

I tried, anyway. I dozed for a while, but found myself unable to fall fully asleep. What had gotten into Dennis? He had never met Geoff and Mari. He knew only a sketchy outline of the story of the collapse of my marriage under the burden of Geoff's alcoholism, followed swiftly by the death of our only child, hit by a car while riding her bike. I had met Dennis after that, while Geoff was still alive, but the loss of Mari had relieved me of the need to have any further contact with him.

Dennis hadn't wanted all the gruesome details; our relationship was supposed to be a fresh start for me. It wasn't that he didn't care, but all that drama and messiness was just a sad, closed chapter, and we were writing a new one.

I rolled over and looked at him, snoring lightly and drooling a little in the moonlight. Dennis had changed when Geoff died, I realized. Subtly and gradually, perhaps, but changed nonetheless. I couldn't put my finger on it, but, once the thought crossed my mind, it could not be dislodged. When Geoff, drunk, had crashed his car—mercifully killing no one but himself—it had had an effect on Dennis, and it was only getting worse.

I had to sleep. Finally, I got up and got a Benadryl and washed it down with wine. As I walked through the dark kitchen, I glanced involuntarily at the portrait. It was too dark to see whether we were all still smiling, but I had the feeling that all three pairs of eyes were following me as I went back to bed.

I couldn't say when I awoke, muddled and cranky, what I had dreamed. All I knew was that Geoff had been there, and it had not been pleasant.

"I dreamed about him," I said over breakfast. "Are you happy now?"

Dennis gave me the strangest look as he slowly finished

chewing and swallowing before he replied. "Was it a good dream?"

"No."

"Not good how? Sad? Angry? Scary?"

"I don't remember. Chaotic and ... unsettling."

"So, maybe I'm right ... about you having some unresolved issues with him."

"Maybe. Not grief, though. Anger, more likely."

"Don't you miss him?"

The question caught me up short; I just stared at Dennis. That strange look was still on his face.

"Do you miss him?" he asked again. Which wasn't quite the same question.

"No." I said at last.

"But you miss Mari."

"Mari was my child! She was a part of me! I will always miss her."

"He was a part of you, too. You were bound to each other by a sacred vow."

"It's not the same."

"Of course not. But ... you chose him, and the two of you consciously undertook to weave your lives together. Mari just happened."

Dennis and I were living together, sure. But, he'd never had a wife or a child. He didn't really understand either marriage or parenthood. I kept telling myself that as I stared at him, unable to formulate a reply.

"Okay, I can see that was the wrong thing to say." He sounded less apologetic than defensive. "But that's more or less how you told it to me."

"We weren't trying to have a baby, but we weren't trying not to, either," I said slowly. "So I suppose you could say that she 'just happened.' But that doesn't have any bearing on how important she was to us."

"I know, I know." He made a placating gesture with his hands. It was a gesture I had seen before, many times, but not from Dennis. From Geoff. I felt a chill and a flush at the same time and momentarily lost control of my face.

"Alison! Are you okay?"

I shook my head slowly, breathing deep as the sensation faded. "I can't have this conversation now. I just … I don't know where all this came from or what is going on with you, but I just cannot."

"Me?" He took his dishes to the sink. "I'm trying to help you."

"This is helping?"

"I'm trying to make sure there isn't some emotional landmine buried in there somewhere," he continued as he turned and pointed at my chest in a way I found unsettling, almost threatening. "Something that's going to go off in both our faces. I want us to be safe from the past, from both of *them*." He enunciated the pronoun with deliberate emphasis and gestured at the portrait as he left the kitchen.

I looked at the picture. Geoff was smiling, but Mari wasn't. Her sweet little face stared out at me with an intensity rarely shown at any point in her short life. She had been such a laid-back, easy-going kid … the emotion I saw was hard to define —there was purpose there, but I couldn't interpret it.

"Mari..." I breathed. "What is happening?"

"I'll tell you what's happening," Dennis said behind me, causing me to jump. He tried to continue, but I cut him off.

"Does the picture look different to you?"

"Different how?" He stepped to my side, dutifully, if somewhat sullenly, studying the photo. I couldn't bring myself to answer the question, to lay myself open to his ridicule, or more questions about the state of my mind. After a moment, Dennis turned to me, and the look his face was distant, closed. "To tell you the truth, I haven't looked at it all that much. I couldn't say if it's different." He gave me a perfunctory kiss and set off to work.

I sat back down at the table, trembling, not looking at the picture. I carefully sipped my coffee and finished my eggs and pretended the picture was not there.

"Sacred vow?" I said suddenly, loudly. Why in earth would Dennis the atheist invoke the power of a sacred vow? The word 'sacred' was not in his active vocabulary.

"What happened to the picture?" Dennis asked over dinner.

"I took it down. It was bothering me."

"Bothering you?"

"I don't want to talk about it."

"You can't just brush it aside like that. Denial won't help."

"Don't lecture me on denial; I was married to an alcoholic."

"Hiding the picture won't solve the problem. It's not working, don't you see? You're just pushing things away, not dealing with them. The picture, your husband..."

"Ex-husband! And you picking fights with me does not

mean I have unresolved issues. You can't just act like a jerk and then blame Geoff, or me, when I get angry."

"Is this how you talked to him?" Dennis countered. "If he said or did something you didn't like, he was acting like a jerk?"

"No, when he lied to me and broke his promises to me and emotionally abandoned me and our child, that ... that was acting like a jerk."

"Do you realize how many times you said the word 'me' in that sentence?"

"Fine. He was a liar; all addicts are liars. He bailed out on the *sacred vow*, and his responsibility to his child. He blamed the world for his problems and hid from his mistakes in a bourbon bottle. Is that better?"

"Oh, come on. So he drank. Was it really as bad as all that? It's not like he cheated on you."

"It is exactly like he cheated on me. He didn't just drink. I drink; you drink. We don't let it interfere with the rest of our lives. When your booze becomes more important than your family, then, yes, that's cheating."

"Did you ever really love him?"

"What? Of course I did! That's what made it so hard." I couldn't believe the direction the conversation had taken. I had never seen Dennis like this before.

"How hard was it, really? How hard did you try to save your marriage?"

"I thought you didn't want to know the particulars."

"Maybe I should. Forewarned is forearmed, and all."

I stood and glared at him. "I do not have to justify to you, or to anyone else, why I divorced him, or explain all the ways I tried to avoid going down that road."

"Sure. As long as you feel justified, why would anyone else's opinion matter?"

"Everyone else's opinion was that I was doing what I had to do, that I had done all I could and more than I should have."

"Everyone's?"

"My family, my friends…"

"People who were already on your side. What about his family?"

"His family was so screwed up, I was glad to have the excuse to sever ties with them. And for the record, his friends, *our* friends, also supported my decision."

"So, everybody bailed on him? No wonder he couldn't pull his life together."

"How do you go from not wanting to know anything about it, to being the world's greatest expert on my marriage … my life?" I was stunned, beyond angry, at the route the conversation had taken.

"How do you go from promising the rest of your life to someone, to not being willing to look at his picture?"

"Fine. I will put the damn picture back, if it makes you happy. And if you really want to know whole story of how it went wrong between Geoff and me, I will tell you."

"No, thanks. I've heard enough. The Gospel According to Alison isn't going to give me the whole story, anyway."

The plate I had taken off the table fell out of my hand and shattered on the floor. 'The Gospel According to Alison' had been one of Geoff's pet phrases, whenever I was reading him the riot act and he couldn't muster an actual defense.

"Alison?" Dennis's voice sounded like Dennis's voice again—I hadn't even realized it had changed until it changed back. For the first time that evening, it held warmth and genuine concern. It wasn't enough.

"Leave me alone," I said, barely able to control my voice. "Leave me the hell alone."

I swept the broken dish glass off the floor, gripping the broom so hard that I almost couldn't unclench my hands when I was finished. Then I got the photograph from the drawer, where I had hastily stashed it that morning, and rehung it. Alien pod-Dennis had been right about the fact that taking it down wouldn't address the underlying issue, whatever it was. Something bizarre was going on. Dennis had become a stranger.

No. Not a stranger.

I recognized the mannerisms, the tactics, and other turns of phrase that had been less obvious than the gospel remark. Having never met him and knowing almost nothing about him, Dennis was acting just like Geoff. He'd almost looked like him at times during our argument, his features taking on Geoff's expressions. Jesus.

Jesus!

I continued tidying up the kitchen, finding one little chore after another to keep me from going into another part of the house and possibly encountering Dennis. I didn't know if I was angry or hurt or scared or some combination thereof, or so freaked out as to transcend all of them. I also tried not to look at the portrait, but once again I could feel the eyes following me.

I got out a bottle of wine, and when I went for a wine-glass, the sunset light flashed on the old, rippled glass of the cupboard door and, unmistakably, formed the word "MOM." I closed the cupboard and opened it again, and again "MOM" appeared in glowing letters.

I whirled around and nearly lost my balance, my eyes locking onto the portrait and almost physically anchoring me as I wavered. The urgency in Mari's face had intensified, as had the hostility in Geoff's. His hands, which had been resting on my shoulders when the picture was taken, were now curled around the curves where my shoulders joined my neck. Involuntarily, my hand rose up as if to brush away the touch I almost felt on my own neck. I stumbled to the table and sat; I put my head down on my folded arms and wept.

At some point, Dennis came in and sat with me, and had the sense not to touch me or say anything. After a while, he poured us both some wine. I tried not to gulp it down.

"Thank you," I said quietly, after the first couple of swigs.

"I'm sorry," he said. "I don't know what got into me."

"I do." I mouthed the words, below even a whisper. Familiar Dennis, my Dennis, was back, but for how long? I wondered. Over his shoulder, I could see Geoff, looking downright malevolent in the dim and shifting light.

I spent the night thrashing around the bed, pursued by images of Geoff and Mari. I was in the car with Geoff when he crashed it. I was driving the car that killed Mari. I was in the car with Geoff when he hit Mari. I was riding my bicycle when Geoff and Mari crashed into me. I was a bystander as Geoff swerved to avoid hitting Mari and hit me instead. At some point, Dennis got out of bed. When I got up to go to the bathroom in the wee, small hours of the morning, I found him sacked out on the couch.

There was a full-length mirror on the back of the bathroom door, almost directly opposite the medicine cabinet mirror. When the door was not quite closed, the mirrors would reflect each other in an infinitely regressing series that was pleasantly vertiginous, like an Escher print. As I opened the door to go back to bed and the mirrors found each other, I found Mari's face in the reflection from the medicine cabinet. I spun around and looked directly at the smaller mirror. I saw only my own reflection. When I turned back to the larger mirror, there she was—her face and mine, side by side by side by side till we merged together towards the vanishing point. Not the baby-face of the family portrait, but her face as an adolescent, as it had been just before her death. Her expression was sad, or afraid, or both. Her hand appeared and rose as if to reach out, and I put my hand up as well, and touched the mirror on the image of her hand. She vanished the moment my fingers met the cold glass. I leaned my forehead against the mirror and pounded it with my fist until it broke.

Then I walked out through the broken glass and went to the kitchen. I stood in front of the picture and studied it. Once again, the image had returned to what it had always been. No, not quite. Now, I was the one who wasn't smiling. Geoff's hands were no longer at my neck, but I grimaced as if they were. I clutched little Mari on my lap as if I were certain of losing her. And I looked like I knew it was all my fault.

"What do you want?" I whispered.

"A decent night's sleep," Dennis muttered from the doorway. I glanced at him, startled, and almost screamed. For half a second, in the dark, he looked just like Geoff, despite the fact that he was four inches taller and had a lot more hair.

"Why is there glass all over the bathroom?"

"They're here," I told him.

"Who?"

"Mari. And Geoff. They're here. They want something from me, but I don't know what it is."

"Alison … you're just upset. And rightfully so. I was a dick; I had no right to speak to you that way. You had a bad dream, that's all."

"I had every bad dream. Dennis … sweetheart…" He caught me as I lurched toward him and wrapped his arms around me.

"This is good," he murmured into my hair. "This will help you put it behind you for good."

"It *was* behind me, God damn it!" I drew away from him, searching his face for shades of Geoff. "I don't know what happened."

"I give up," he said tiredly. "Obviously, I can't talk to you about this, and one of us had better be able to go to work in the morning." He kissed me on the forehead and went to the bedroom. I almost followed him, but curled up on the couch instead. He could have the bed to himself; I wasn't getting any rest, anyway. Every time I slipped into sleep, it was into another horrible image of myself, Mari, Geoff, and death. In between, I lay awake trying to make sense of it. What was it all about? What did they want from me? The answer was getting clearer.

"Augh!" Dennis came hopping out of the bathroom on one foot, pressing a washcloth to the other and cussing. He had forgotten about the glass on the floor, and so had I.

"Was it too much to hope that you might clean up after yourself? Jesus, Jupiter, and Krishna! Get me the Band-Aids, would you?"

I brought Dennis the first aid kit and started cleaning up the glass shards. I remembered stepping on them and checked my own feet for cuts. I was almost disappointed I didn't find any. I felt a sudden urge to run my fingers along the sharp edges, to enfold the jagged pieces in my hands and squeeze until the blood ran between my knuckles. It was all I could do not to slash myself then and there.

That was what they wanted. They wanted me to suffer, as they had suffered. They wanted me to bleed. They wanted me to die.

"Listen, Alison," Dennis's voice came from the other room, sounding much more distant than it was. "You need to straighten your mess out, whatever the hell is going on here. If you don't want to hear what I have to say about it, then figure it out yourself."

"I know," I called over my shoulder. "I know," I repeated, whispering.

By the time I was finished in the bathroom, Dennis had left for work. There was a note on the kitchen table from him. At least, it had his name at the bottom. The handwriting was very distinctly Geoff's, as was the tone. The content was no different from what Dennis—or Geoff, speaking through Dennis—had been saying for the last two days.

I hadn't looked at our old photo album since I didn't know when. I fetched it from the hutch and sat at the table and pored over the images. Page after page. Most of the pictures were of Mari, because Geoff was taking most of the pictures and I didn't like having my picture taken, and she had been the most precious, adorable, amazing thing in the world, anyway. I touched her face a hundred times, trying to summon the memory of the feeling of her skin.

When I looked up, I was no longer surprised to see their faces gazing back at me out of whatever glass happened to be in my field of view. Mari looked frightened and Geoff looked angry. Mari was questioning and Geoff was demanding.

How could you let this happen to me?

How could you do this to me?

Why didn't you save me?

Why didn't you stop me?

What makes you think you get to go on with your life and be happy, after what happened to us?

Mari's face took on the same hard, cold, accusatory expression as her father's, an expression it had never held in life. She had always resembled him more than me. Their faces, hovering in the glass of the windows and cabinet doors, were now almost identical.

"No, Mari, no," I moaned, and reached out, curling my arms around the memory of the child who had sat on my lap in the portrait studio. Mari's phantom faces sneered, mocking me, before merging with the faces of her father. It wasn't Mari at all, I realized; it couldn't be. It was only Geoff, using the image of our daughter to torment me. Had she ever been here? Or had it all been Geoff, that vindictive bastard, hitting me in the only place where he could still hurt me?

It didn't matter. The damage was done. The question could not be unasked, and knowing that it had been all Geoff and not Mari didn't change much. I didn't need them to ask me accusatory questions, because I was already asking them. I had been all along.

I was in the bath with the razorblade in my hand when Dennis got home. I hadn't put the thin little blade to my flesh yet, but I had already taken a handful of pills, just in case I lost my nerve when it came time to cut. I was still contemplating it, nursing a bottle of wine, when he came into the bathroom.

"Hi, honey," he said quietly, in a voice I never thought I'd hear again. "I'm home."

"Please don't stop me," I said thickly, my lips getting numb. "Don't let anybody save me."

"I wouldn't dream of it," he replied. "Far be it from me to interfere with what you want."

"It was my fault."

"Yes, it was," he agreed matter-of-factly. "All of it was your fault, wasn't it?"

"I know." My voice went all thin and squeaky, as if I were about to cry, but it didn't get past the throat-achy part. My vision was getting blurry, but his face also seemed to be changing.

"You never thought about me, did you? It was all about her." There was a terrible, bright, white light growing in the mirror behind him, turning his head into an indistinct blur. There was something in the light, a shape that became clearer, more distinct, as he became less so. Another face…

She filled the mirror and flowed out of it, so exquisitely beautiful that I wondered how I could have been deceived by Geoff's miserable counterfeit. She smiled, setting off what felt like a harmonic vibration throughout my body. I closed my eyes for a moment, waiting for her touch, and almost couldn't open them again. When I did, she was no longer looking at me. It wasn't me she had come for.

When she spoke, it was the most unearthly sound, but not really a sound…

"Daddy."

No-Longer-Dennis turned, made a strange choking noise, and flung up one arm as if to shield himself from her. The light engulfed him. Then she was gone and the light with her.

Dennis crumpled to the floor, miraculously not hitting his head on anything. At some point, without any conscious effort on my part, the razor had bitten into my arm. I barely noticed. Her smile was burned into my retinas and my ears rang with her voice. I felt myself sliding deeper into the water. I heard something like a groan, but faintly, as from a far distance. Someone said my name as my head slipped down and the water closed over my face.

Then an arm slid beneath my shoulders, and I was lifted out.

Stepping into October
William Pack

SHE DIED on an unseasonably cool, dreary, June day. A series of mini-strokes eroded my Great Aunt Bernice down from a spry, sharp old gal to a shadow. Leave it to her to surprise; I fully expected that she'd make October and her 90th birthday. She lived an October life. Whether by accident of birth or choice, nearly every moment of any significance to her seemed to be confined to those thirty-one Fall days. Recognizing death's prerogative, October followed her into June so she could die on an October sort of day.

It was 1984 and I was sixteen. I was closer to Aunt Bernie than to any other in our family despite the distance between our ages. Her stories spanned the years. She filled my head with wonders and dreams and more than a few nightmares. I loved her for the peculiar family lore she shared, like how the ghost of her late husband, Uncle Joe, once saved her life, and for the other world she purported to live in full of shadowy dark corners and mysterious goings-on. I loved her because the stories may have been false, but she told them true.

We buried her on a Friday. That weekend, my parents made a list of chores that needed doing at her house. Maybe I was conscripted into service because I had the summer off, nothing but idle time and no say in the matter, or maybe it was because her unusual house never creeped me out like it did the rest of my family.

Aunt Bernie had lived in her Bridgeport neighborhood home for over sixty years, half of those as a widow. Built as a workingman's "two flat" in 1850, my Uncle Joe rebuilt, remodeled, and expanded the place to the point I doubt a single board remained from the original structure.

It's most unusual feature was a Chicago-born oddity. The foundation was laid before the city engineers raised the streets to accommodate the modern sewers that would save the growing metropolis from its own filth. Instead of digging down to install the pipes, an impossible feat in the swampy earth, workmen laid the pipes atop the streets and covered them over. At the same time, most buildings were raised to the new street level—if you could afford it. The original owner couldn't—so this one house, on this one block stayed below, a lasting reminder of his place in the world. The first floor sat twelve feet below the street level. A concrete bridge crossed from the sidewalk, over the front yard, to the converted second floor main entrance. Chicago's older immigrant neighborhoods are dotted with such homes.

My family thought the house "strange," and "bizarre." It was. So was I, so I loved the place. For everyone else it had the unnerving effect of a funhouse mirror, their world temporarily distorted into an unnatural shape.

With so much to do, I asked my parents if I could sleep in the house for a while. I mean … why spend so much of the summer running back and forth between the two houses? I don't know if they really believed it, but the argument worked. With enough bologna and frozen pizzas, I could have a few friends over, get things done faster, and not lose too much of my summer.

Dad dropped me off Sunday night to start work Monday morning. Settling in for the evening, I turned on the TV and switched over to channel 7 for the Sunday Night Movie, *Invasion of the Body Snatchers.* Not the 1956 original—the creepy 1978 Donald Sutherland remake, featuring an extremely creepy Donald Sutherland. Just as his character had found Brooke Adams' pod person and he was trying to save the "real" Brooke, I heard a soft noise...

Tap. Tap-tap-tap.

I thought someone was knocking on the front door. When I opened it, Poe from sophomore English popped into my head—*here I opened wide the door, darkness there and nothing more.* I made a note to replace the lightbulb. Turning back into the room, again I heard a noise, *somewhat louder than before.*

CLACK. Clack-Clack-Clack.

It came from above, in the attic. Something metallic, but deeper. I turned off the TV and concentrated.

CLACK. CLACK.

It got louder, harder. Hard enough that the ceiling vibrated right over my head as if someone hammered at it from the other side. I didn't know what it was, but it didn't sound good.

CLACK. Clack. Clack. Clack.

The knock faded, as if it moved farther away. I tried to imagine a mundane cause, maybe a loose shutter flapping in the wind. I frowned. Something seemed off with that theory. I'd have to go up to investigate. The thought that I was living one of Aunt Bernie's stories nagged at me. I pushed it away. The noise could be an irate bird or a rabid squirrel or—

(damn it, Bernie)

something worse.

Clack. *Tap*. Clack. *Tap*. Clack. *Tap*.

A rabid squirrel with a wooden leg?

The stairs leading up to the attic were at the back of the house through an enclosed porch. As a child, I'd climb the half level of stairs pretending to be a detective, then turn the corner of the switchback discovering a secret passage leading to the lair of my imaginary arch rival. I'd heave open the heavy hatch-like door and save the day. Now this brave detective feared having to confront a bird. I peered up the stairs. The trap door in the floor of the attic was already open.

I flicked the light switch. The light from unshaded bulbs flowed out the opening, down the stairs, just to the tips of my shoes.

The odd knocking sound stopped.

It must be stunned by the lights … *whatever it is*. I went back down to the kitchen and grabbed my weapon of choice, a broom. Nothing said, "SHOO" better than a swing of Aunt Bernie's trusty O-Cedar.

The attic was large and ran the full length of the house. I could stand to my full height in the center with plenty of room to spare. As spacious as it was, I felt claustrophobic. Aunt Bernie, helped by Uncle Joe, had packed it full of cardboard boxes and cast off furniture, an odd assortment of a life's accumulation of things, leaving only a narrow aisle stretching from one end of the attic to the other.

Lying off to one side was a weathered green door with a brass knocker in the shape of an Irish Claddagh, the original front door that my German uncle replaced when they moved into the home. A couple of beat up steamer trunks were stacked to one side. They looked like they were dragged the entire way from Germany when my ancestors immigrated. Another part of Aunt Bernie's stories that became part of me.

The window at the back of the house was secure. I opened it to look outside. There were no shutters at the back to catch the wind. In fact, there was no wind.

I walked toward the street side of the house, poking the broom handle in the spaces between the trunks and the boxes. The thought of rousing a frothing rodent terrified me, but less appealing was trying to sleep with something—

(damn it, Bernie)

some *thing* rampaging above my head. The window at the front of the house was also secure and shutter free. As I started back, I whacked a couple boxes with the broom, sending up puffs of dust.

Nothing moved.

Halfway back, I stepped into the cold spot. There have been perhaps four times since when I felt what came next, when I have accidentally stepped into a space occupied by something—or someone—unseen. This was the first, but it didn't matter, no previous experience ever prepares you for that moment. It is always sudden, always surprising.

Every nerve came alive—pins, and needles, pins and needles. What it might feel like to be electrocuted. A wave of every possible sensation flooded me all at once. Not painful in any normal way, but so cold it burned. Goosebumps. A cold sweat. Teeth-rattling chills. My hand locked around the handle of the broom, unable or unwilling to drop it. My bladder suddenly too small. My lungs suddenly too large, impossible to fill with enough air. My vision distorted, stretching and squeezing the room like carnival taffy. I thought I might pass out. The air thickened, muffling all sound. My mouth went dry and tasted of copper, like pennies, like death.

At the same time, there was a moment of exhilaration like coming out of a stifling house into an October breeze. Pure excitement flooded me with adrenaline. Suddenly, I realized Aunt Bernie's ghost stories seemed true because they were *true*. I couldn't believe this was happening. It chilled me and warmed me at the same time.

This happened in a moment, in the second biggest city in America, on a middle class neighborhood street, in a house that I now knew to be haunted. I stepped into the October Aunt Bernie lived in every single day, an October that straddled life and death. Then October was gone and blind panic hit.

It came on as sudden as a morning alarm. I was awake again. I could feel my limbs, yet, I couldn't move. And believe me, I wanted to.

Then, I heard Aunt Bernie's voice. Not out loud. It was a

fragment of a memory, from one of her oft-repeated stories. *Don't let it in, let it through.* She gave me a key to unlock the panic, as if she knew I'd need it one day. I forced in a breath.

When I exhaled, my oxygen-starved breath hung in the air like it was an Arctic night.

Ok, I told myself. You're just startled, not scared. Someone just wants your attention. I repeated it until the panic that clenched my insides unwound. I jumped back, staring at the spot on the floor where I had just stood. Then I looked past the spot, at the hole in the floor where the stairs led down, out of the attic. I needed to get there.

I sensed a shadow twitch at the edge of my peripheral vision, but when I turned my head it slithered out of view. Whatever it was had my attention. It was time to let it know.

"Who are you?" I creaked, my voice raspy.

I listened and waited. Already, the pain and panic had become a disembodied memory, as if it were a story Aunt Bernie told me about someone else.

Then it hit me.

A large ... *something* ... brushed by me, and brushed hard. Not something random, not like a gust of wind; it moved with will and purpose. I half turned from the blow and staggered to my right as it came from behind me—from the front of the house—and headed straight for the back. The hatch door at the top of the stairs was thrown shut.

It wanted to keep me in the attic.

Boxes fell from one side to another, swept over by invisible arms. I crouched and put my hands up for protection. Something wrenched the broom from my hands, broke the handle in two, and flung it aside. The discarded green door began to shake and rattle as if someone or something desperately wanted out of some non-existent room behind it and into this existing one. The Claddagh knocker hammered out the familiar ... CLACK-CLACK-CLACK.

Suddenly, in one swift and violent motion, the door flipped over, spun, and hit the floor with a wood splintering CRACK!

Everything stopped.

My legs unlocked and I rushed to the stairs. Just before pulling up on the door handle, I paused. I had the strangest feeling. I put my hand on the door and froze, straining to listen. My heavy breath counted the seconds. I had the feeling that someone was standing just on the other side.

Remember how it was when you were young and playing hide-and-seek? You'd be in a room looking for someone and yet, even though you can't see anyone, you just know someone is hiding there. Just *know*. You *feel* it. That's how I felt.

I could wait no longer. I grabbed the handle with both hands and hefted the door. It didn't resist. No one, no-*thing*, hid behind it. I went down and into the kitchen. I stood there, not sure what to do, gasping for air, my heart racing.

TapTapTap

"Shit." My eyes went wide.

TapTapTap

I swallowed hard. Just air. After a moment of disorientation, I realized the knocking was coming from the door—the front door.

It was Maggie, the neighbor from across the street. As Aunt Bernie aged and her children scattered, Maggie had acted as her unofficial caretaker. She was a stiff prig who dressed like the warden of a women's prison, but she was good and kind to my Aunt.

"I saw the light on in the attic. Is everything okay?"

"Sure," I lied, "Just fine." My mouth felt like it had been swabbed with cotton and left to air dry. I felt a little light-headed, almost feverish, and very, very thirsty.

"Okay," she said. "Just, you look—"

"Everything's fine."

She paused. "Okay, if you need anything I'm—"

"Thanks. Yes. Yes. I'd better get the light. Thanks." I closed the door.

Well, I thought, at least she didn't say, "You look like you've just seen a ghost."

I went and shut off the attic light. I poured two glasses of water and sat on the couch. I felt as if I'd been emptied of all will. Exhausted, I could barely move. Leaving was not an option. How would I explain this to my parents? Besides the thing in the attic seemed to be done for the night. How did I know? I didn't. I felt it.

I fought sleep, trying to stay alert. I turned on the TV and hoped I would not get sucked in *Poltergeist* style. I flipped the channels, one after another, a mindless, almost hypnotizing activity. One minute the channels were racing by, the next, I woke to the morning after a dreamless sleep.

My body was refreshed, but my mind was still on edge. For the first time ever, I wanted to be out of Aunt Bernie's house. Mowing the lawn would temporarily help solve that problem and give me time to think.

39

Why didn't she tell me the stories were real?

I noticed in the grass lay a dry red-orange leaf as big as my hand, a ghost of October past or a harbinger of October yet to come. I shredded it with the mower, running over it twice.

Did she try to tell me or did she want me to discover it myself?

Ahead another autumn leaf floated on the tips of the unmowed grass. This time it gave me a shiver. It was freaking July 2. I wondered if I just inherited a life in Aunt Bernie's unending October.

The first indication that anyone was behind me was when I felt a hard, strong hand clamp onto my shoulder. I gasped. How was I to defend myself without the broom? I whirled around and there was Maggie, staring at me over the top of her glasses.

"Damn it, Maggie!" I put my hand over my mouth, now more shocked at myself than Maggie.

Her manner was sharp, curt; she clearly had no time to scold me for my expletive. "Did you see him?"

My jaw hinged open like Wile E. Coyote's.

"You know what I mean. Did you see him in the attic?"

Lying was no longer an option for me. "I ... no. There was ... something. I felt something. Something cold. And hot. I felt—"

"Sick, like you had a fever."

I shook my head. "Almost ... not so much. More thirsty. Really, really thirsty."

"I could tell last night. Had it written all over your face. I told your Aunt he was trouble, but he never really bothered her. You know how she loved her ghosts."

"I always thought they were just stories."

"Boy, you got some surprises waiting for you."

"Do you know who it is?"

Her lips got very thin as they tightened. "I wish I knew. Bernie said he had always been here. The original owner, maybe? He supposedly died in there. There were stories. Some old timers in the neighborhood said he wasn't in his right mind. Roamed the attic raving, ate rat poison. I heard a story that he got influenza, or maybe cholera, and the family quarantined him in the attic to die. Someone else said it was rabies."

"So you've seen something?" I asked.

"No, but heard him more times than I care to tell. He doesn't mind me much. I've been helping Bernie so long, he must think I'm a spirit. A few say they seen someone in the window, staring out. Most only hear him."

"The doorknocker."

"That's what got you all upset, him knocking about? He must like you. Late at night, when the house was empty, people have … I have … heard screaming from the attic. Wild screeching. Mostly he cries for water, as if—"

"He's thirsty." I interrupted. "And Aunt Bernie lived with it? Didn't she want to know more?"

She shook her head like you do when dealing with a child that just refuses to stop touching the hot stove. Her expression became stern. "No, don't need to!" She poked me in the chest with a crooked bony finger. "Bernie told me sometimes *not* knowing is good for you. Ever think of that?"

"I … I don't—"

"Well, *do think*. Meanwhile, you've got chores to do." She turned and hurried back across the street. Then over her shoulder she yelled, "And stay out of the attic!"

The rest of my stay—and, yes, I did stay—was quiet. I now have my own story to tell. (Thanks, Aunt Bernie—I think.) I'm still not sure if knowing more is better. Always meaning to, I never learned any more about the house. I've come to understand, though, that October isn't so much a page in a calendar as it is a state of being existing in strange off-kilter houses and in shadows that move just out of vision's grasp.

October means living in a world where things that aren't real become stories that are.

Maggie has been dead for twenty years now. After the house was cleaned out and sold, Maggie and I occasionally exchanged letters. In her last one, she wrote that Aunt Bernie's former house had burned down. No lives lost, nobody injured. After a series of very short-term tenants, the house had gained a "reputation." It was vacant after that for a number of years.

She said that a man in the neighborhood called out, raising an alarm, waking some of the neighbors. They saw an eerie red glow behind the windows and called 9-1-1. By the time the fire department arrived, the house was beyond saving. The only thing they could do was to stop the flames from spreading. After an investigation, they believed the blaze was electrical in nature. How that spontaneously occurred in an abandoned house remains a mystery. The inspectors suspected arson by a person or persons unknown.

During the investigation, the police and firemen tried to find the man who had first raised the alarm. There was no trace of him. None of the neighbors would admit to it. None could identify him. They said they hadn't seen anyone, only heard a man yelling.

They said he'd been shouting for water.

Green Lady
Lynne Handy

IN 1848, I wed my second cousin, Easton Pound, and left my London home to sail to his in America. The trip across the Atlantic was uneventful except for the sea dragon that surfaced near the coast of Ireland. I awakened early that morning, went up on deck, and saw the emerald isle basking in an absinthe glow, and there it was—a sleek, black creature floating on the water. Its three humps gleamed like wet tar; its head was flat, shaped like a serpent's. Easton joined me at the rail and, when I pointed the dragon out to him, he said it was a trick of light and the lapping waves.

I turned to face him. "You're mistaken. I've seen such creatures before—two, in fact, when I traveled to Brazil with Papa."

He made no reply and when I looked back, the monster had returned to the murky depths. I knew then that Easton's education was rooted in only what he knew, and his lack of open-mindedness would tax my patience. Still, I'd married him and I cogitated on what that might mean as we made our way by ship, boat, and carriage to Pound Hill, Easton's estate.

I'd known Easton all my life, and I rather liked him. Ten years my senior, he was neither tall nor thin-faced like most of the eligible men I knew, but actually my own height, five feet eight inches, with a muscular physique, broad welcoming face, and dark brown eyes. His father, Caleb, was dead, and so was his mother, but his stepmother, Grace, lived with him, as did two young cousins, Lemuel and Justice, whom he'd brought from England.

After his parents' deaths, Easton returned to London for annual visits. On my twenty-fifth birthday, he came to my house and devoted an entire afternoon to boasting about his three hundred and sixty acre farm in Pennsylvania and his plan to breed Arabian horses. As he spoke, I thought his farm might be an excellent place to rear children. I looked at him anew.

That day, he praised my beauty, adding, "Your interest in my endeavors has awakened my love. When I return next year, I'll ask you to marry me."

I thought he was joking, but as it turned out, he meant it, and when he proposed, I was another year older, Mother was hovering, and so I accepted.

A word or two about Mother: she thought I'd never marry because I had foresworn submissiveness. Women's low place in public affairs sorely vexed me. Female suppression, I believed, began with the Ancients blaming Eve for Adam eating the apple. Did she pry open his mandible and shove it in his mouth? Ha! Eons later, the Apostle Paul solicited women's financial support for his Cause and then refused to let them speak in public! Hypocrite! That brings me to religion—at thirteen, after reading Voltaire's *Candide*, I became an atheist and sent a letter to the *Times*, condemning religious faith as a substitute for rational thought. The editor published it, which caused a stink in our social circle. Mother didn't leave the house for weeks.

Fortunately, my late father ensured that I was schooled in theories of the great thinkers and encouraged me to speak my mind. Aware that I might find marriage disagreeable, he set terms upon my dowry favorable to me and not to my spouse: one-quarter was payable after the wedding ceremony, with the other three-quarters payable after two years had passed. If I left my husband then, I'd receive the remainder of the dowry. Papa also stipulated that if I agreed to remain in the marriage, I must take my children with me to his law firm to release the funds to my husband, who would not be present. This was to prevent an unworthy husband from holding my children hostage. Papa understood men's greed.

As for the farm Easton brought me to, it was fine enough; the house was a three-storied brick structure with a gambrel roof and a coach house, a lawn large enough for a vegetable garden and two flowerbeds of irises and peonies. Outbuildings included a barn, two stables, and numerous sheds for storing plows and hayracks. He built the newer stable with the first dowry installment.

Two years now, I've been at Pound Hill. Country life is pleasant, but I sorely miss the opera, plays, and discussions with people who've read something other than *The Farmer's Almanac*. The town, ten miles away, is growing. People are building houses, and a few years hence, there will be a more diverse community that includes persons of taste and means.

Today is June 1. Mother Grace, a great strapping woman who looks like she should be yoked to a plow, is napping.

Easton and his nephews, Lemuel and Justice, are overseeing the livestock. I'm *enceinte*, due in six months, and at odds. The doctor has forbidden horseback riding, or even traveling over roads in the carriage.

I step outside to admire the irises, then hear the strange trill of a bird and, keeping to a well-worn path, follow the sound into the woods. I grow excited. A glimpse of the creature will allow me to find its name in Mr. Audubon's book.

The path ends. Thick green canopies obscure the sun. Grasses, as tall as my shoulders, impede my progress, but the birdsong still beckons. Gathering up the hem of my skirt with one hand, I push through the underbrush with the other until I stand on land that once was cleared, but is now overgrown with weeds. The bird is silent now, a disappointment. Moving forward, I discover the foundation of a cabin no larger than my closet, a crumbled chimney, shards of glass, and a charred door. A squirrel dashes from beneath a half-burned slat to scurry up a tree. I lift the slat and find a child's dirt-encrusted, wooden rattle, shaped like a tiny barbell.

Soil clings to the toy. I wipe it off with the hem of my skirt, slip it in my pocket, and turn to survey my surroundings. A stream runs near the cabin and I wonder what it's called. A row of pines grows south of the stream—at least, what I think is south. In vain, I look for the opening to the path. Then, the grasses move and I stiffen.

A wolf?

When Mother Grace's collie, Shem, appears, I gasp with relief. "Here, Shem," I call.

He runs to me. I scratch his ears.

"Good boy. Take me home."

Shem leads me back to Easton's house. Mother Grace, dressed in black bombazine, sits on the porch in a rocking chair.

"How was your nap?" I ask.

Shem puts his front paws in her capacious lap and she rubs his head. "Refreshing," she replies. "Did you go for a stroll?"

I show her the rattle. "I found this at a burned-out cabin."

"Throw that filthy thing away!" she cries, shrinking as if I've shown her a vampire's tooth.

"What happened there?" I ask, placing the toy on the porch railing.

"You were at Trapper's Creek. A woman and her bastard died there."

"How sad. How long ago was the fire?"

She stares at the ground. "Fifteen years or so ..."

"What were the names of the woman and child?"

"She was a Scot. Called herself Clara Frazier. Don't know the bastard's name."

We sit in silence. I ask no more questions. For the rest of the evening, even at dinner, when we are joined by Easton, Lemuel, and Justice, Mother Grace is uncharacteristically quiet.

Easton notices. "Mother Grace, has the cat got your tongue?"

"I have dyspepsia."

"Perhaps you ought not to be having a second helping of pork," he says.

She doesn't reply.

Lemuel turns to Easton. "Was the stray bull calf at Mrs. LeGrand's farm?"

Mother Grace scoots off her chair and stomps from the room, nearly stumbling over Shem, who lies in the doorway.

Easton stares after her and shouts for the hired girl. "Mercy!"

Mercy comes into the room at a trot, her white blond hair straggling from beneath her white cap.

"Go see to my stepmother. She seems unwell."

Mercy bobs a curtsey and runs upstairs.

Easton turns back to Lemuel. "The calf was in Mrs. LeGrand's orchard. He got through the fence near the stile."

"We'll fix the gap in the morning," says Lemuel.

After dinner, Easton repairs to the porch to smoke his pipe and the young men depart for the stable to bed down the horses. Mercy comes downstairs.

"How is Mother Grace?" I ask.

"She's better," the girl replies. "I gave her some bitters." She goes to the kitchen.

I feel tension in the house, seemingly stirred by my questions about the fire. Pacing the parlor, I pass the window, where I see Easton on the settee, looking out into the twilight. I step outside. The rattle is still on the porch rail and I pick it up.

"Easton, I found this toy at Trapper's Creek, where Mother Grace said ..."

He grabs the rattle and hurls it into the shrubbery. "Don't go there again."

His behavior stuns me. "But why not?"

"There are wolves in that part of the forest. You're fortunate you weren't attacked."

"But the fire—what caused it?"

"Don't speak of the fire ever again," he says, coming close. "Do you understand?"

His saliva sprays my face and I recoil. "Easton, you're frightening me."

"I'm thinking only of your welfare—and our child's."

Shaken, I go upstairs to my bedroom, which I no longer share with Easton. For the duration of my pregnancy, he is sleeping in the south bedroom. I pass Mercy, who casts me a sympathetic look. I am fond of the girl, whom the Pounds pay only a pittance. I have given her some of my clothing and shoes. Later, someone taps on the door. I open it, and Mercy slips inside and pushes the door shut.

"You mustn't talk about the Frazier fire," she whispers. "It upsets the Pounds."

"I see that, but why? Tell me about Clara Frazier."

Mercy wrings her chafed hands. "Clara took up with the trapper that lived in the cabin. He left, never came back. A year or so later, she birthed a boy. The father was a mystery. The cabin burned one night with her and the baby inside."

"How dreadful."

"A terrible thing," Mercy says, casting her eyes downward. "Some say her ghost haunts the clearing, but I don't believe in ghosts."

"You would have been a small child when it happened..."

"My folks talked about it." She leans closer. "Some say it was the baby's father that set the fire to hide his sin. Somebody set a boulder against the door, so it wouldn't open."

"Murder is the greater sin," I say, after a moment.

"There's no accounting for what men do in a passion," replies Mercy. "If the man had a wife who ..."

I stare at Mercy. "I see."

But I don't see. Not yet.

A week passes. Easton apologizes for frightening me, but I am cold. The memory of his features distorted in rage, his spittle spraying my chin, disgusts me. I see how he runs his farm. Everything is well-oiled and his is the master hand that controls it all. After my child's birth, I may not stay at Pound Hill.

A London friend sends John Stuart Mill's latest book, and having read the introduction, I'm eager to delve into the first chapter. In the side yard is a hammock, which I find inviting, so I settle into it, open the book, and am immediately distracted by the strange birdsong that led me to Clara Frazier's cabin. I steel myself. Curiosity will not lead me into the forest again.

The discarded rattle lands hard on my stomach. I rise too quickly, spill out of the hammock, and sprawl on the ground, my hands cradling my belly. I hold my breath, assessing my condition, until I'm certain the tumble has not set in motion any internal disturbance for my baby.

I get to my feet. An eddy of dust swirls around me, raising the hem of my skirt and flipping the pages of Mill's book, which was also flung to the ground. Gripping the rattle, I hasten into the woods and, push through the tall weeds, until I stand at the ruins as if in a trance. A hawk flies overhead. His cries alert me to where I am and I run back to the house.

The next day, I return to the ruins, thinking Clara must want the rattle returned. I lift the slat to replace the toy, but it's as if the space is full and won't accept it. Thrusting the rattle in my pocket again, I return to the house.

Over the next several days, I steal away to Trapper's Creek again and again, drawn by associations to Clara: birdsong, thoughts of the fire, and the weight of the rattle in my pocket. On one occasion, I encounter Cousin Justice, a boy of sixteen with tousled brown hair.

His mouth is downturned. "Easton wants us to stay away from here," he says, "but I feel Clara's spirit and come to pray for her."

"I feel her too," I say. "Tell me, have you seen her?"

"No, but men say she was a small lass with green eyes and red hair."

Justice bows his head. I leave him praying in the sun.

Now that I have a description of Clara, I conjure up visions of her tiny frame, large with child, delivering him alone in the small cabin, bearing him in her arms to show him the wonder of sunlight, bluebirds, and clouds. She challenges my notions of the soul, heaven, and hell. If her spirit is wandering, where *should* it be? Is there an afterlife? Why is she earthbound? If she and her boy were murdered, does she seek vengeance?

With a child growing in my womb, I understand well the implications of maternal affection. I've felt my baby move and I'm on the verge of loving it. Hesitation comes from worrying that she—I think of her as female—might not survive, that the delivery will be so strenuous that it will kill her or me. I dream of Clara's desperation when flames leapt around her and she couldn't open the door, and then I see myself giving birth to a sickly child who refuses to suckle. Oh, I wish for Papa, who made nightmares disappear.

I sit on the porch, smelling the red roses that cling to the trellis.

"Are you all right?" Mother Grace asks.

"Yes, quite," I say.

"You're how far along now? Five months?"

I nod my head.

"I wasn't fortunate enough to have children," she says. "If it weren't for Easton, I would never have known the joys of motherhood."

Has Mother Grace felt joy? Her face is so sour I can't imagine it.

"How old was Easton when you married his father?" I ask.

"Four. What a darling he was." She pats my belly with a large, rough hand, an intimacy that annoys me. "You're carrying a fine son for Easton. You'll make him proud."

Easton also inquires about my health, and since his inquiries always come after his stepmother's, I know they discuss me. Once I overhear Mother Grace ask my husband if he's seeing Mrs. LeGrand, a buxom widow, for any reason other than to discuss the hole in the fence. I don't hear his response, but I hear hers: "You're just like your father."

A few nights later, I sit at my bedroom window, held spellbound by the full moon. In the yard, something moves. It's a woman, dressed in green, flitting from the willow tree to the fence. I lean forward to see who it is, but blink and she's gone. The next night, I see her again. She darts toward the outdoor pump and then—poof!—vanishes. She is small, slender. Her hair appears bound up in a bun. Is Mercy wandering the grounds? I put on my robe and go downstairs. Taking care to not disturb the household, I open the kitchen door, step onto the back porch, and wait for the woman to reappear.

A bat flies from a tree and I shrink into the shadows. A horse whinnies. Above, someone raises a window—probably Easton worrying that a predator has broken into the stable. After a moment, the horse quiets and Easton closes his window. I turn to go in the house when a sudden motion catches my eye. The woman is by the willow tree. She is not Mercy. She unpins her hair, the color of bright copper, and it falls to her hips. Her eyes gleam like those of a lioness. My heart constricts.

"Clara," I say.

She fades into nothingness.

I sit on the steps and hold my head in my hands, for I wish to assist this restless spirit who died violently, unable to save her child. I want to help her move on to wherever the dead go. Returning to the house, I lie in my bed, thinking of Clara with her blazing hair, seething eyes, and green dress. The green dress stirs my memory and I rise to consult a book on Scottish myths. Under "Glaistig," I read of a Scottish spirit, ambivalent in nature, which sometimes protects children and cattle herds, and at other times, wreaks vengeance on evildoers.

Closing the book, I know I ought not to believe in ghosts, since I was schooled in rational thought, but if one is to dare to know, as Kant advised, nothing can be ruled out. There may well be a parallel universe in which restless spirits roam—I've actually seen the physical manifestation of Clara Frazier. Ghosts do exist.

Why does Clara choose to reveal herself to me, but not others? I return to bed, resolving to question Justice more thoroughly before he goes to the fields.

The next day, I find the boy at a shed where he's oiling wagon wheels.

"I've seen Clara's ghost," I say.

His eyes flash a warning. "Lemuel says I'm not to speak her name again. He says when I talk about her, I give her permission to haunt."

It's not my intent to bully Justice, so I leave, but I reflect on what he said. Perhaps it is better for Clara—and for me—if I don't seek her out.

October. I'm in my seventh month of pregnancy. Mercy has expanded the waistlines of most of my dresses. I feel sluggish. My breasts are sore. The baby is restless. I've named her Rose, for there is nothing more beautiful. Easton pats my shoulder as I pass by, but I still don't trust him. One night, I hear him leave his bedroom and later, look out my window to see him riding his stallion, Brutus, westward. He's off to see Mrs. LeGrand. An hour later, the dining room chandelier crashes onto the walnut table. Shem barks.

Mother Grace cries, "What is it, Easton?"

"He's not here," I say.

She comes to her door in her nightgown. Lemuel and Justice exit their bedrooms, tucking nightshirts into their trousers. Justice brings a kerosene lamp and we hurry downstairs. Only I think to wear slippers and so they all halt when they see broken glass inside the doorway. Mercy and the cook appear. I take the lamp and examine the broken chain.

"One of the links broke," I say.

A cold wind chills my spine. Clara. Could it be she who pulled down the chandelier?

"The links seemed fine yesterday," says Mercy. "I dusted the chain with the feather duster."

Lemuel says testily, "You must have pulled it apart or ..."

Whoosh. A green spear with jagged edges strikes my abdomen with great force and I nearly drop the lantern, but Lemuel reaches out a long arm and grabs it. I cross my arms protectively across my womb, convinced the spear was aimed at my baby. Clara Frazier wants my Rose, either to assuage her grief or to seek vengeance. I am seized with violent spasms. Justice runs across broken glass to catch me as I sag to the floor, and I lean against him as he guides me into the parlor. I sink on the sofa. The tremors continue. I bite my lip, feeling the force of a vengeful spirit.

Mother Grace and the young men are solicitous. They, of course, did not see the spear, and think my labor has begun. Lemuel helps Mercy cover me with a shawl while Justin picks glass shards out of the soles of his feet, the result of his sudden rush to my side. In the midst of this commotion, Easton appears in the doorway.

"What happened?" he asks.

Mother Grace upbraids him. "You should have been here. The chandelier fell. It upset us all, especially your wife. I fear she's gone into labor."

Easton takes my hand. "Is it true? Is the child coming?"

Pain convulses my body. I don't answer. He gathers me in his arms. The spasms cease and I fall asleep. When I awake, my head is on my husband's lap and he is snoring lightly. I smell drink on his breath and the scent of jasmine on his shirt. I remember Clara Frazier's aggression toward Rose, and Easton's embrace, which may have made the pain stop. Is he more powerful than Clara? Did he sire her child? Was it he who set the cabin afire?

I must know.

I rouse Easton with a nudge. "Husband," I say, rising to a sitting position, "we must talk."

He does not interrupt when I tell him I've seen the ghost of Clara Frazier, but instead fixes me with smoldering eyes. I conclude and wait for his response.

"You were hallucinating," he says impatiently. "Ghosts don't exist. Remember when you thought you saw a sea dragon? It wasn't there."

I start to tell him Justice has also sensed Clara's spirit, but change my mind—why involve the boy?

"Did you father Clara's child?" I ask.

He glares at me. "No."

"You ride off to Mrs. LeGrand's with regularity and come home smelling of her. It's a conclusion that comes to me logically."

His face reddens. "We won't speak of this again."

"Then I swear I will return to England with my baby after she's born."

His eyes widen. I can well imagine he's thinking what the

loss of several thousand pounds will do to his plans to fill the new stable with Arabian horses. He leaves the room.

The sea dragon was there. I saw it.

The first snowfall occurs in late October. My condition forces me into lethargy and I don't require much mental stimulation. I read, play checkers with Justice, and nap. Mother Grace brings me a book from her personal library: *The Mother at Home or The Principles of Maternal Duty*, written by a Massachusetts preacher. I fall asleep over its dreary pages.

Now and then, I walk into cold spots and know Clara Frazier is stalking me, but I do my best to ignore her by freeing my mind from dangerous associations. Upon feeling the cold, I tell myself the house is drafty, that Easton needs to stuff more wadding around the windows, or that my blood is thin, allowing my bones to chill.

Two days before Christmas, I'm in my sitting room, watching sleet spatter needles against the window pane, when my water breaks and I rush to the door to call for help. Mercy, who had been sweeping the hallway carpet, drops her broom and hurries to my side. Mother Grace, seeking out Mercy to scold her for the abandoned broom, bursts into the room, sees the girl fastening me into a nightdress, and goes to summon Easton.

He bounds into the room, looking wild. "I'll send Justice for the doctor."

I make a weak protest. "The sleet—"

"Justice is an able horseman. I'll send him on Brutus. He can ride along the river road—it's protected by trees."

By evening, I'm well into labor, and Justice hasn't returned with the doctor. I will say this for Easton, he is in and out of the room, repeatedly offering help, but I have no time for him. The business of birthing Rose seizes me at my core, and I seek only Mercy's ministrations. When I'm burning up, she throws off the sheet and fans me. When I ask for water, she gives me sips from a porcelain cup. When I reach out my hand, it is hers I grasp. She's told me she helped her mother safely birth three children. I trust her.

After hours of agonizing pain, my labor stops and I know from the expression on Mercy's face that this cessation does not bode well for my baby. Still the doctor hasn't come. Easton worries that Justice has been attacked by seditionists who sometimes raid from Maryland. Mercy places her ear on my abdomen and listens for the baby's heartbeat.

"Little Rose is resting," she says.

The tautness leaves her face. Much relieved, I tell Easton to join his stepmother and Lemuel for dinner.

"Will you be all right?" he asks.

"Mercy will call you when my labor begins again."

He leaves the room. I listen as his muffled footfalls sound on the stairs. Mercy rests on the daybed near the chifferobe. As sleet hits the window, I think of Justice, hoping he's safe. I begin to nod, drifting on the edge of consciousness, seeping into a black void where…

Then suddenly, I'm aware. I'm falling into a pit of utter blackness, which smells of blood and excrement. I gag, flail my arms. My nails rake the sides and scrape up vile substances. My heart beats like a Congo drum. From far away, someone calls my name. The voice grows louder. Death is coming for me.

But there's Rose! I can't let myself die. If I do, she'll never take her first breath. Clawing my way out of the death hole, I try to call for Mercy, but though my mouth opens, no sound comes out.

Clara Frazier appears. Her eyes flash fire; her red hair wraps over me like a shroud, tightening around my throat.

"I'll take your child as she did mine!" she shrieks.

She?

I break free of her hair and give it a hard yank.

"Old Caleb Pound sired my Johnny!" she screams. "His barren wife threw a lantern in my window and blocked the way out."

Mother Grace.

I try to push Clara away. She is air—there is no substance to her. She uses her hair like a whip, lashing my abdomen, my breasts, and it is then that I feel Rose start to birth. I cover my privates with both hands, not wanting her to come with Clara there to snatch her away. The spectre attacks me again. I hear her hiss, smell her acrid breath, and cringe from the pain of her blows.

Then I hear Justice's voice, warning me not to give life to the ghost. Closing my eyes, I will Clara from my consciousness and concentrate on Rose, who is emerging from my body. I squat on the floor, and with one great surge, she slips out, pulsing and bloody. I catch her in my hands.

"Mercy!" I cry.

Mercy leaps from the daybed, grabs the scissors, and cuts

the umbilical cord. Then she helps me back into bed as I hold Rose fast against my bosom. When I search the room for Clara, I see she's slunk into a corner, thwarted by my indifference.

"Don't leave me," I tell Mercy, needing her faith in the here and now.

Only when Easton returns, does she go downstairs to fetch water to bathe Rose and me.

"A girl," says Easton, frowning, just as Mercy returns with the water.

Clara crouches in the corner, uneasy with Easton there— and Mercy, too, for neither believes in ghosts. She is shrinking.

Two days pass. Clara is still here. Her skin has turned gray and her hair has lost its luster. Even her green dress has faded. I hear knocks on the outside door. Then, voices. Easton comes to say a farmer found Justice in a ditch, riddled with bullet holes. The farmer brought the body with him on a sled and Mercy is washing it. I burst into tears.

Easton frowns. "There was no sign of Brutus. A good Arabian, lost."

I look at Clara's corner. She's gone. It was propitiation from the Pounds she wanted. Justice's life would do.

He had prayed for her.

I weep long for Justice, a sweet, kind boy, regretting that I didn't dissuade him from trying to help Clara move on. Lemuel builds a pine box for his brother, who will lie in it in the coach house until the ground thaws. Shem howls for Justice's return. Mother Grace asks to hold Rose, but I tell her no. She is a murderess. When Easton protests, I tell him his stepmother is clumsy and will drop the baby.

I will say this: if one dares to know—as I did in allowing Clara Frazier into my consciousness—there can be repercussions even on innocents like Justice and little Rose. Easton, Mercy, and Lemuel, with their firm hold on reason, kept the spirit away.

I don't think I will ever be a ghost—not because I don't believe in heaven or hell—but because spirit lore is not part of me. No doubt, Clara grew up with the old beliefs.

Easton speaks of going into Maryland after Justice's killers, but I think he wants only to find his horse. Whatever he does, I don't care, for I've informed him I'm returning to England next month with Rose. I'm taking Mercy, too.

"Will you come back?" he asks.

What a fool he is to ask.

What Happened at the Lake
Wren Roberts

VERA PUT on her lipstick last, before eyeing herself in the mirror. Her brown hair needed a cut and her eyes needed more sleep than she could find time for, but she was as ready as she was going to be. The precious few minutes in the morning that belonged only to her were about to end. She swallowed hard, stealing herself for whatever the day would bring before leaving the quiet of her bedroom.

It wasn't that the rest of the house wasn't quiet. It was just a different quiet. The quiet of the house filled the air with awful dread that something was amiss. She crept down the stairs. Out of habit, she closed her eyes at the step that squeaked. She paused outside of the boys' playroom, like she did every morning, to listen.

The playroom was supposed to be the formal dining room, but necessity had demanded other plans. After Jacob had been born and diagnosed the same as his brother had been, it was too much letting them play on another floor. Really, everything was too much, but Vera learned that you expanded yourself to fill the life you were given. Even if that meant stretching yourself so thin you barely seemed to exist at all.

She wobbled at the silence on the other side of the wall.

Every now and again, a grunt came from her older son, Lem. She remembered being the mom with one autistic son, and how difficult that had been. Then, when she was the mom with two autistic sons, people seemed to whisper behind hands and give her sidelong glances at the park.

"I don't know how you do it. I could never do what you do," was what they always said to her face. What had she done? Grinned and beared it. So she'd say "You just do what needs to be done."

They said other things behind her back, when they didn't think she could hear them.

"Poor Vera and Adam."

"How unlucky for them. How hard their lives must be."

"I think I would kill myself if I had all that to deal with."

"Bad luck."

"Bad genes."

"Bad vaccinations." They were never as sneaky or discreet as they thought they were.

Sometimes, late at night, after the boys were finally too exhausted to be awake anymore and she herself had found her bed, Vera would think about the life she could have had. The life without the bad luck, bad genes, and bad consequences. The life where her sons had blossomed into the boys they could have been: happy, social, neurotypical. A life not ruled by routines and schedules, not filled with doctor visits, therapy visits, and sensory diets. In the dark, she could almost admit how badly she wanted that life. The one where she wasn't trapped with her two children and their disorder.

But now she wasn't a mother of two children on the

spectrum. No. Now there was the autistic one … and then there was the dead one. Her terrible wish, the one she didn't really mean, had somehow manifested itself into this unwanted reality. She hadn't yet been back to the park to pretend not to hear what the other mothers said about her now.

As she listened to her living son, Vera played out in her head what was going to happen next. This part had been the same every day for the last two horrible weeks. She would go into the playroom to greet her son. He would be playing in his own little world, and he would see her and screech a little. His eyes would drift wildly about the room. He would ask "Where's Jacob?" in his disinterested monotone. Then, he would ask over and over again, getting more and more agitated each time. The queries would be rapid-fire, and she wouldn't have a chance to soothe him before he got worked up. Finally, Vera would kneel down beside Lem and tell him Jacob wasn't coming back. Lem would start shrieking and knocking himself in the head with a curled fist. She would hold him so tight she wouldn't be able to feel herself cry.

She didn't know when the terrifying routine would change or when it would feel different.

By the time they finished their little meltdown, it was past any reasonable time for breakfast. Schedules were important, and she would not forgive herself for this lapse. She was Mom with a capital M. She was supposed to be the rock that kept her boys' shores safe from choppy waters. Here she was, falling apart herself. Here she was, the woman who had failed to keep her son safe.

After the funeral, the priest had told her it would never get better, but it would someday get easier. Someday hadn't come the next day, or the next day, either. Every day, Vera found herself taking her deep breaths, closing her eyes at the squeaky step, and waiting outside the playroom before she gathered her strength and walked in.

Lem was sitting far too close to the muted television. His forehead practically rested on the screen. His fingers occupied what little space was between his eyes and the TV, flickering around in some game Vera had never figured out. The family called it pepper-grinding. He laughed the throaty, jerking chuckle that would have been more appropriate for a man of fifty, not her ten-year-old boy.

"Mommy," he said. He always sounded far away when he spoke. He didn't turn to look at her, but he always seemed to know when she was in the room. "Where's Jacob?" he asked, it almost lilting like a song in his rhythmic monotone. "Where's Jacob? Where's Jacob? Where's Jacob?"

His torso rocked and twisted. He rolled his head back to look in her direction, upside-down, before the rest of his body turned to put him upright again. He had the toothy grin she loved so much.

"Oh my sweet Lemon," she started. She wondered if today would be the day, the day they could both start to move past that other day. She blamed herself for not watching them as closely as she knew she should. This had been her wish, had it not? But it was also hard to not blame Lem, even though he didn't know what he was doing. He didn't understand what the consequences would be. He didn't know pushing Jacob into the lake would kill him. He didn't know what it meant to drown.

But he had done it. He had done it. They were partners in this crime. Someday she would need to tell him. To confess her complicity. Would it be today? Should it be today?

"Where's Jacob? Where's Jacob? Where's Jacob?" He was getting more agitated. His grey eyes were sliding faster and faster around the room, looking for his younger brother.

She desperately wanted to put off telling him Jacob was gone, to hold off the cries of "Why? Why? Why?" and head-knocking. She knelt down on the floor the measured distance she always did, so he could come to her. "Jacob's not..."

His eyes stopped searching, which took Vera by surprise. His eyes never stopped when unsettled. He hopped to his feet, his mouth oscillating between the gross mimicry of upset and that toothy grin. Back and forth; upset and happy. Arm and hand suddenly pointing over her shoulder.

"There he is!" He did the rigid jump-clap he did when happy. His fingers snapped back up to his eyes, grinding pepper. He made his happy noises. "There he is," he echoed, barely engaging his voice.

Vera looked at her son doing his celebration ritual. She didn't even think about not looking over her shoulder. She had to know what amazing thing had snapped him out of his pre-meltdown.

There was nothing there.

They should have sold the house with Lem's diagnosis.

Living in a house backing up to a lake was playing with fire. Children on the spectrum drowned all the time. Vera and Adam had talked about it, but they loved the house. There were two of them, one parent for each son. They could handle it. They would never let their children meet that fate; they would be careful. Jacob's diagnosis a year later hadn't changed anything either.

Now, Vera wished she could go back in time and get rid of the house. She would trade anything to have her son back. Adam had suggested they move a couple days after the tragedy, but how could they move now? This was where Jacob had lived, had filled their lives with sunshine and sorrow. This was where he had died. They couldn't leave now, Vera insisted. She couldn't leave her baby behind. Even if every time she washed the dishes that meant looking out where she had found him floating face down.

There weren't as many dishes anymore, which she tried to tell herself was a small relief, even if it killed her inside. Instead of washing three dishes after lunch, now it was only two. She, too, relied on their routines, and even this small shift was devastating. Devastating in a way Lem didn't notice. Couldn't notice.

She was just putting the second dish in the rack when she heard him speak.

"Mama, I'm done," a voice said, just like Jacob always said. Her heart skipped a beat, her mind not yet registering that son was the dead one.

She whipped around, ready for the nightmare to be over. But it was just Lem, holding out his empty glass of orange juice. Of course it was Lem. It could only be Lem.

"Mommy, I'm done," he echoed, sounding so far away.

Her heart fell into the pit of her stomach. She forced a smile. "Thank you, sweetie," she said, ignoring her disappointment.

"Thank you, sweetie," he echoed. "Can we go outside today? Outside?"

Vera bit her lip. They hadn't gone out to play since the accident. But she couldn't refuse Lem with his eyes sliding out towards the backyard. "What will we play?"

"With Jacob."

A deep breath, eyes closed. There could be no tears. "Lemon Drop, I told you: Jacob isn't here. He can't be."

Lem crossed his arms and pounded his foot on the ground. "No!" He stomped again, his Velcro sneakers making a satisfying stamp on the linoleum. "No! I play with Jacob. In the backyard. In the backyard!" His face twisted into the mask he wore when he was upset. He squeezed his eyes shut and stomped his feet yet again.

She couldn't deal with another meltdown right now. Not in the kitchen, and not over the backyard. "Okay, okay. We'll go outside. In the backyard."

Vera slid her feet into the moccasins left by the back door. Someone had moved them there for her, perhaps her mother or Adam. They were the perfect shoes for running outside quickly. Like when you find your son in the lake. It was weird, Vera thought, how she could put them on again, like it was nothing. They were just shoes, and they were miraculously dry.

She held out her hand for Lem. He took it in the delicate way he did, before clamping down on it too tight, like he also did. Hand in hand, they slipped into the backyard. She couldn't take her eyes off the water. It was calm and smooth like glass. She consciously kept the bad memory at the edges of her consciousness. She wasn't ready to deal with that yet.

Meanwhile, Lem had dropped her hand and was skipping through the grass after a pale, white butterfly. It had taken him years to learn that movement, and though it was still jerky, it was functional. Jacob's movements had always been more fluid. He had been higher functioning, as the therapists and teachers and doctors liked to say. He was the one who she didn't have to worry over as much. Or at least she had thought. He had looked her in the eyes most of the time. And he laughed when she made a joke, and it didn't sound like a pull-string toy. He was more interested in the world around him. Curious, even.

How had Lem gotten so close to the water all of the sudden? It was going to happen again. Her blood ran cold and she momentarily froze, even though she knew what she should be doing. Yet her voice was caught in her throat and her feet were rooted to the ground. God help her, it was going to happen again. Lem was dipping a sneaker into the water's edge.

Finally, her adrenaline kicked in. She sprinted down the yard, screaming his name. "Lem! Lemuel! No!"

He jumped in, sinking down to his knees. He laughed and bent over. His hands threw the water up and he gleamed and cooed at the droplets. He took a step forward just as she hit the lake. She reached out and grabbed his arm. He yelped and jerked it away, giving her an indifferent "no." He took another step forward into the lake.

Tripped.

Plunged into the water.

Screamed.

Panicked.

Vera wrenched her son up above the surface. For a moment, she swore it was Jacob she was saving. But Lem came up laughing and crying and fighting to make her let go. There was no way on heaven or earth she would let him fall back into that dangerous water. She clutched him to her chest and had her daily cry. Together, they sobbed and sobbed and sobbed. And Vera did her best to ignore the pleas of her dead son. The quiet "Mama, I need you," whispered directly into her ear, burning its way through her skull.

They would have to sell the house.

Adam came home for dinner, which was unusual. After eating in silence, he had taken Lem-duty, which Vera was grateful for. She had needed a break, but she didn't have the words to ask for one. Lem needed his father, but Adam had been withdrawn and unavailable since Jacob's death. It was good to see them together again. She tried her best to ignore the big empty hole where Jacob's giggles should have been.

She had to leave after a while. The emptiness had spread out and covered everything like a wet blanket, dampening any enjoyment she could have over their renewed connection. She took her mug of chamomile tea outside, and was soon surprised to find herself walking around the side of the house to the backyard.

She looked out at the small houses across the lake. Their windows reflected as ribbons of light on the calm water. Twilight was settling over their small village, and no one had taken their boat out in weeks. Normally there were a few families enjoying the cool evening air at this hour with a leisurely cruise, but they seemed to have collectively decided to refrain for now. She wasn't sure if it was out of respect or horror.

Her son was out there, somewhere. The water had been cold that afternoon, but it didn't compare to the chill that clung to her bones when she thought of how he had just spoken to her. Or when she remembered the way he floated face-down, with Lem giggling from lawn, pointing.

"Jacob?" She whispered. She walked down to the shore. She didn't know what she was doing; she wasn't sure if she wanted him to answer. "Jacob?"

The stillness that answered was enough to crush her heart into nothingness. Lem had seen him. He was there; he had to be. She stumbled on a hidden hole in the ground. She dropped the mug and didn't notice tea splashing her leg.

"Jacob?"

She looked back at the house. Maybe things would be different if Adam were watching. But he wasn't. He was in the playroom at the front of the house. He was with Lem. One parent for each son. Like they always did when Adam was home.

Vera barely even noticed the water when she ran out of

land. The mud sucked at her moccasins, and she left one behind. The bottom dropped off quickly, and her hands glided against the mirrored surface.

They had never the let the boys play in the water. The only times they went swimming were in pools with life vests and floaty wings. There the water was clear, and life guards watched her children with almost the same intensity that she did. The lake had never been a point of interest, except at night when they could watch the reflection of the moon.

"Jacob?"

Something was out on the water, something she hadn't seen just a moment ago. It didn't have much of a shape, but it floated right at the surface. She pushed forward, even when the water came up to her shoulders. Even when her tippy-toes no longer skimmed the bottom, or even the plant life that lived there.

Somewhere along the way, she lost her other shoe.

She swam to where she was certain she had seen something floating. Nothing was there, and scanning the water proved fruitless. She turned around and realized she was much farther out than she thought. Almost in the middle, really. The water was cold. She should head back, she knew. But … her son.

Something cut through the water nearby. It circled around faster than she could keep track of it.

"Jacob?"

She could almost hear him breathing. It was like he was right behind her, but each time she looked, he evaded her. He was playing hide and seek. Jacob had always loved that game, and it had been a nightmare breaking him of the habit in stores. Here in the water, she forgave him. She would play with him forever, if he would just come home.

"Mama, I'm cold," he said.

"I know, baby. Me too."

"I don't want to be alone."

She looked back at the house. She thought of Lem shrieking with laughter with her husband inside. Adam was a really good father, she thought. One parent for each son. It was the only way.

The New Girl
Kate Johnson

I DON'T know when he'll come to me, or how. Usually it's just his voice in my head, dreamy and fluid, the sound resonating inside me the way music can when the harmony's just right. Sometimes it's more than that, but only for a flash. A boot disappearing around a corner, a hand reaching to knock over a stack of napkins. I don't know why that scares me more—it should be worse feeling him inside me—but somehow the image of that boot or denim shirt cutting across the corner of my vision unnerves me in a way his voice does not. But I never see much of him. By now I'm certain he sees everything I do, and he's watching me. Studying me.

So I can't use the rest room, at least not at the sub shop. Instead, I run two storefronts down to the bank, where they have enough foot traffic not to notice me ducking inside once in a while, a safe place to close a door and know that no one's watching. By no one, I mean him.

I didn't know about him when I got the job. I was just a nervous sixteen-year old, looking for work because my mom was only part-time at Menard's and my brother had moved in with his girlfriend. My timing was perfect for the owners of the shop; Mike's nephew had quit without warning, leaving them in the lurch. Annie studied me across the counter. I wasn't much to look at: skinny, pale, with dark hair that wouldn't commit to a style. I wore nice clothes, but they were Goodwill. Nothing came together on me, anyway.

"Usually we hire older kids, college kids," Annie said. "But you say you'll stick around during the school year, and work after classes?"

She was the first person who had looked at me that day. I felt my head bobble on my neck. "Right. We … I mean, I … need the job." I made myself hold her eyes. Hers were blue and kind. Mom eyes. I don't know what she saw in mine, but, after a moment of hesitation, she gave me the job. Tuesday through Saturday, ten to nine with a goofy three hours off mid-afternoon I didn't know what to do with, because other than Annie and Mike, I knew no one in town. We'd just moved here, it was summer, and, other than work, I had nothing to do.

The job turned out to be a good one. Annie and Mike were nice and it was fun building sandwiches. After a few weeks, I knew orders for the regulars by heart and could make smoothies faster than Mike. This was around the time they gave me a little raise and trusted me with a key. I'd never be opening the shop myself—prep for lunch was too intense—but I started closing up. The last two hours were usually slow, so around seven, they pulled off their aprons, repeated instructions I knew by heart, and left to spend time with their two kids at home, rug rats permanently stuck on peanut butter and jelly.

That was when he first came to me. Almost closing time, about a quarter to nine, while I was wiping down the counter. It was August, the tail end of twilight, that weird time when you feel the changing of the guard somehow. That transition from light to darkness, from sharp edges to shadows.

"Lucy."

I stiffened. Before I could form a thought, even to be afraid, every hair on my body rose.

"Downstairs…" The voice and the feeling entered me. It wasn't my feeling. It was his. Loneliness. Longing. I recognized the feeling, going all the way back to preschool. Like kids forming a ring at circle time, leaving me out to form the tail that turned their "O" into a "Q." A feeling of not belonging and knowing it.

"Lucy, I'm downstairs." Stronger now. I got a fleeting, fuller sense of him. Confident. Playful. A rule breaker. Then, he was gone.

I leaned on the counter to keep from falling. This kind of thing wasn't exactly new to me, though; I'd heard voices and even seen things before. My mom had taken me from doctor to therapist to psychiatrist years ago until her credit card maxed. I ended up on medicine for a while, but pills couldn't keep them away because they came to me, not me to them. Never, though, had the feeling been this strong. His loneliness, his longing mingled with mine, along with something else I couldn't identify, something that was new to me, and that scared me. Maybe I could close a few minutes early. I glanced at the wall clock. 9:20. A chill entered me and didn't ease until I locked the door behind me.

I didn't go down to the basement of the shop much. There's something inside a person that knows not to spend time underground in a cold, dark, windowless space. I'd run down to grab cup lids or pickle jars because Annie and Mike stored dry goods there. But I'd come back up quick, only taking a moment sometimes to touch the uneven, limestone walls or feel the grooves worn into the hard-packed dirt floor. People had walked down these stairs for a century and a quarter, grabbing bags of flour or salt or sugar. It had always been a shop of some sort: a grocer; a butcher; a baker. A smoother wall ran along my left as I ran down the stone stairs, where someone had started laying mortar over the limestone, then stopped. It extended down the wall, into the shadows. Over the years people had written their names on it: Gustav Kiefer 1898; Stefan Olson 1916; Oscar Steiner 1937. I'd wonder over them for a moment, think about sticking my own name somewhere on the smooth surface, then run back up.

The next day I went downstairs during my break. I gave my eyes extra time to adjust to the dim light and studied those names. There were dozens written randomly, with no attempt at chronological order. Even Annie and Mike had written theirs a few years ago, with a "2008" following behind. Cold pressed against me as I got closer, back and toward the bottom of the right corner.

He spoke quietly. "That's me. 'Timothy Quinn '85.'" Written with a black laundry marker in a large, bold scrawl. I rested my fingers on it and felt that cold again, colder than the wall should be. Goosebumps covered my body.

Before I could make for the stairs, he spoke again. "Lucy, don't be afraid. That's me. Please don't leave." A warmth fought the coldness now, a softness, his longing, his need.

Without thinking, I knelt down and rested my cheek against his name. I felt the cold and the rough mortar against my skin, and that new feeling filled me. I didn't recognize the name of it yet, but I would soon enough. My heart pounded, my blood pumped. My fear was different now, and not the fear of a ghost haunting me. It was a fear of whatever had made me lay my cheek against his name.

Who was he?

I hurried upstairs, feeling him close to me, but not inside. I grabbed my sandwich to spend my break sitting by the river, but somehow it had become 4:50. My break was nearly over. I walked in the rest room and felt him, alert and watching. That was the first time I ran to the bank for privacy.

Eventually I found my courage. "Did anything ever happen in that basement?" My voice squeaked, but Annie didn't notice. Timothy had just knocked an order off the counter and she was picking it up, no doubt assuming vibrations from the door closing had caused it.

She tilted her head. "Could be. The building's old enough. I heard they used the tunnel as part of the Underground Railroad, unless that's just legend."

"Tunnel? What tunnel?"

"The one behind that little door, in the very back. Where the extra chairs are?" She stabbed the check on the receipt spike. "They used to deliver coal through there, down a chute from the street. Of course we don't need coal anymore. But there were tunnels down there, they used to link up a lot of these old buildings. To me it seems like a great place for, I don't know … a kidnapping, or a murder, or … Hey, am I scaring you? I'm sorry! My imagination's too big."

"No, I'm okay." On the word 'murder' my body had gone cold. I heard Timothy, hurrying to tell me it was okay, it was no murder.

"Are you sure, Lucy?" She was looking at me harder.

"Yes," I answered, because I had learned years ago not to say "no" when adults asked if I was okay. Nothing good could come of it. In that shadowy world that brushed against my own, no human could help me, anyway. Ask Annie to call the cops? Have them arrest Timothy for breaking and entering? All I'd accomplish was losing my job, maybe not right away but fast enough, and I needed the job. I liked the job. I liked Annie and Mike.

"Anyway, they filled the tunnels in, back in the nineties, I think, when they dug up the road to lay sewer pipes or cable. Whatever it is they run. Our tunnel doesn't go back very far now, maybe ten feet, then you hit a dirt wall. We checked it out when we bought the place, in case we could use it for storage. But it's too damp. Too dark. Too … undergroundy." She gave me a little shiver just for fun and I gave one back for real.

When they left at seven, I ran downstairs. By now I kept a penlight in my pocket to help pierce the darkness because I liked touching Timothy's signature, and feeling that odd new feeling fill me. This time I walked past it, in deeper than I'd ever wanted to go, and looked around those chairs. I pulled four away and discovered the outline of a short door made of old, rusting steel. It was a funny little door, more of a hatch, wider than tall, barely big enough for a person to fit through.

It hinged at the top, so that opening it meant swinging the door up. There was an old 2 x 4 lying on the ground, I guessed to prop it open, and an ancient shovel leaned against a chair, probably for the coal. I bent down and examined the latch at the bottom. It had a hole for a lock but there wasn't one, and a hole for an index finger. I slipped mine in and pulled up. It was rusty and sticking, so I squeezed harder, then heard the bell ring on the door upstairs. A customer.

Relief.

Disappointment.

Relief.

Then a brush with Timothy as I passed his name, him sighing, "Your skin looks so soft." He stayed with me until I reached the counter.

School started up. It was a new school with new kids, but I paid almost no attention to it, except for the few minutes I spent in the library.

"Hi, I'm new in town," I said. "I'd love to know more about its history, its legends and stuff. Like stories about the settlers and the tunnels they built under Main Street?"

I could see no one had expressed interest in anything to this librarian for a while. She clapped her hands. "What a marvelous idea! I know just where to look! Follow me." She led me to a shelf dedicated to the Fox River Valley and dug out a book on the history of Main Street. Score. I grabbed others with promising titles, checked out fast, and got to math class late. Lunch followed. I navigated the cafeteria line, then found a seat at the end of a table of kids like me, loners who didn't talk much. Life ran smoother when I didn't.

Now I started work at four. During my new break, from 6:30 to 7:00, I sat by the river and pulled the books from my backpack. I'd expected them to be boring, the way history books usually are, but these weren't. Maybe because I'd seen the door and met Timothy. Or maybe because no one seemed to know much about the tunnels, like who built them or why, and the blanks had been filled in with legends. I read they'd been used for runaway slaves, then later for bootleggers. An old-timer insisted Al Capone ran a crime syndicate down there, and another told the story of a bank robber who hid himself there for years before turning himself in, half-dead. I read about a sicko who'd kept a woman chained down there for weeks before her brother found him, and killed him with his bare hands. There was a photo of the creep, long dark hair and gleaming eyes, even scarier than the photo of Al Capone. I shivered and hugged my knees.

Then I got to the part where they filled in the tunnels and I found what I'd been looking for. In 1988 the state gave money for Main Street to be modernized. Section by section, the old street was ripped up, pipes were laid, and the old tunnels were backfilled with dirt. While all this was happening a group of teenage boys, led by the mischievous son of a town baker, climbed the safety fence to explore one night. A tunnel collapsed and Timothy Quinn, age sixteen, was trapped within. His friends tried to dig him out with their hands, but were finally forced to call the police and confess what happened. By the time he was uncovered, he was dead.

There was a color photo of him. I looked at it closely. Eagerly. Maybe because all the others had been black and white, his photo leapt from the page. He had straight blonde hair lit by the sun and a wide smile. I couldn't tell his height, but he was slender. He looked fast and poised for action. I wondered if his voice back then sounded the same as the voice I heard now. He was the kind of boy I would look at secretly, the kind I guessed would never look back.

In real life.

I touched his face with my fingertips, then traced down further, along his body, to his feet, which were barefoot in grass. The odd new feeling came over me again and I couldn't blame it on him because he was back in the shop. I felt it curl my toes and spread heat as I looked—looked—*looked* at him. I had a longing, too. Not just for a friend, though I had none. This involved my body and now I could name it.

Desire.

Didn't that just figure? That I would fall for a spirit attached to no body instead of a body attached to a spirit. I sighed and shut the book, looking instead at the wide, deep river. The tunnels had run under even it. Now the tunnels were buried, he was buried, and the relentless water swept over it all. So had time.

"Just in case you hadn't noticed, that's the fourth time that boy's come in for a milkshake this week, when Dairy Queen's right down the block and cheaper." Annie was looking at me, her head tilted.

I hadn't noticed. I glanced at the boy, who was standing outside now, waiting for the light to turn green. "He's in some of my classes."

"Imagine that." She rinsed the scooper. "He's kind of cute, don't you think? He doesn't have a dad, either. But I know his mom, she's real nice. They both work at the t-shirt shop."

I nodded. I hadn't thought about whether he was cute or not. I hadn't thought about him at all, and I'd be surprised if he was thinking about me. With the greatest of care, I'd torn Timothy's picture from that book and I kept it in my bedroom, in the drawer of my nightstand. Besides, our ice cream was better than Dairy Queen's. I understood anyone thinking it was worth an extra eighty cents.

"How are you liking the kids at school? This is a pretty nice town, I think." She was such a mom. Still looking at me, her brow wrinkled. I looked back, and nodded again.

"They're great." I told her what I'd told my mom last week, "I'm hanging out with a girl from my lunch table Sunday."

I saw her body relax. "That's fantastic! Grab the cookies before you leave Saturday, anything that doesn't sell."

I smiled and gave another nod. Last Sunday I had done something new. Because the shop was closed, I used my key to sneak in the side door, careful to leave lights off, and went down to the basement. Down there it was okay to turn on the light, though it was only a bare bulb that swung overhead, not bright enough to reach the corners. I had brought my penlight and some WD-40. I pulled aside those chairs and sat down Indian-style on the hard-packed dirt. I sprayed the latch and squeezed and squeezed until finally I felt it giving. Timothy spoke words of encouragement.

"Lucy, thank you. I've been so lonely…" A brush against my arm, so light it only touched hairs.

86

"I think about you all the time, Lucy … I wait for you."
His breath on my neck, my body shivering.

"I wish I could be with you. Lucy, I *feel* you…"

I felt him too. Inside me or sweeping against me, a chill that didn't chill, but warmed me instead. I sat on those stone steps whenever I got the chance and allowed him inside me, deeper each time, until afraid, I ran back upstairs, back to work. Then I became worried that Annie and Mike were noticing. Time to invent a lunch table friend.

At last. I felt the latch gliding smoothly under my finger. I scrambled to my feet, held it tight and pulled up. And pulled, and pulled again. I felt the click of it unlatching, but realized the steel door itself had swollen with rust. Disappointed, I sat back down and examined it in the fading beam of my penlight. There was no way to tell where the door stuck, metal upon metal. Maybe the entire perimeter. I needed something, like a metal file, to slip inside a loose corner and work around the frame. Before I could even look around for a tool, my flashlight went out. Not gradually like I'd thought it would, but suddenly. I jumped to my feet.

"Please don't be afraid of me, Lucy. That wasn't me, that…"

But he couldn't reassure me. The overhead lightbulb threw nothing but shadows back here. Shadows that were moving for no reason at all. I hurried off, not pausing near his signature. As I raced to the staircase, I saw a denim shoulder disappear around a shelf, and I shuddered. At the top of the stairs I shut off the light and slammed the door.

My dreams alternated now between a fear that twisted me

in my bedsheets and a desire I didn't know what to do with when I woke, sweating and yearning, his name on my lips. I pulled myself dreamlike through school, not waking fully until I got to Annie's and felt the dream slip inside me, fulfilling me somehow. Then everything fell back in place and I greeted people cheerfully, built sandwiches and made milkshakes, running downstairs eagerly to fetch anything needed. I was okay once I was in the shop, and better in the basement. But the tunnel called to me behind that rusted door. I knew it was my destiny.

My mom didn't keep tools and there weren't many in the sub shop. Mike's narrowest screwdriver didn't dig in nearly deep enough. But I eventually discovered that by slipping a sharp knife between the door and frame and hitting the blade with a hammer I could work my way slowly around, inch by inch. Hour by hour. I couldn't do this during work, of course. Or even on school days, because I needed to get home. But on Saturday nights and Sundays, providing I came up with a good story for my mother, I snuck away to work on the door. I broke blades and ran to Goodwill to buy more cheap knives.

By Halloween I was halfway around. I celebrated by taking a black Sharpie down those stairs. Next to "Timothy Quinn '85," I wrote "Lucy Mallory '13." I paused, making up my mind. Our names were written on a badly-lit section of mortar. I took the Sharpie and put a "+" between them.

He hit me fast and hard. I lost my balance, tipping breathless on my back.

"Lucy, I *love* you…"

I dusted myself off and knelt back down. I leaned forward

and placed my lips on the "Y" of Timothy and lingered there. Resting my forehead on the scratchy mortar I whispered, "I love you, too."

Winter came with November. A bitter wind blew in with customers and I shivered over every scoop of ice cream. Mike claimed I was too skinny and pressed me to eat more during break. I was the first at school to come down with the flu. I missed a week of work because I had to, though I ached for Timothy, and touched his picture so often the fabric of the paper wore through. Annie ran over with soup and met my mom for the first time, who was embarrassed, because our apartment was a catastrophe. I could see through my fever that both their smiles were forced. When I returned to work, Mike gave me a fifty-cent raise. I flushed, thanked him, and grabbed a cloth to wipe the tables.

Mike and Annie were going away the entire week of Thanksgiving and closing the shop. During their time away I would succeed in opening that tunnel door. I tried to hide my excitement, but Annie noticed it. She thought I was happy to have the week off, which made her happy, too.

"Have you made plans for the holiday?"

"Yes." Of all things, I blushed.

"Oh my God, Lucy—do you have a date?"

"Kind of," I admitted. Which was the truth.

"We want to meet him." I knew why she was saying that. She'd been unimpressed with my mom, which was easy enough to be.

I flushed redder. "I … maybe. Someday." The bell rang over the door and I hurried to the counter.

When we locked up Saturday, a lengthy process because we were locking up for a week, Mike pushed fifty dollars on me. I made an effort to refuse, feeling it was charity, but he insisted.

"You're the nicest employee we've ever had, Lucy. Take this … to make up for the lost work week. Consider it a paid vacation." He pressed it into my palm. "Use it to have some fun." He hesitated. "Go out with some girlfriends. Or buy some awful jeans I'll yell at you for wearing to work."

I grinned. He kept a running commentary on what teenage girls wore. "Okay, I'll make you sorry you gave me this."

We laughed and stepped outside. The wind grabbed the smile from my face and flung it down the street. Annie locked the door. They left for Duluth; I left for home.

But not for long. I spent Sunday writing my term paper for English, but, when my mom came home from work, I said I was spending the night at a girlfriend's, because school was off for the week, too. She asked for a name and a number and I made them up, jotting them down on a slip of paper, because I knew the last thing she wanted to do was check up on me and find out I'd lied. She poured a tumbler of wine and took the paper, then kissed me goodbye. Before I left I saw it fall on last night's pizza box.

It was even colder and windier than the night before. I huddled inside my jacket and listened to the discount knives rattle against each other in my backpack, a steady rat-a-tat

marching beat as I hurried to the shop. I slowed down when I
got close, pausing in the dark to make sure there were no
witnesses as I opened the side door, and slipped inside.

He is waiting for me. Maybe he always is, but it's more
apparent now because the shop feels so vacated. "Lucy …
your face is glowing. How I missed you."

"Well, I'm here now," I answer. Loud and clear, because
Annie and Mike are five hundred miles away. I pause, then
admit it. "I missed you, too."

I can feel him smile inside me. "I love you."

My voice is softer now. "I love you, too."

"Come to me."

I'm already descending the stairs. The small bulb seems
brighter because my eyes are already adjusted to the night's
darkness and the closed shop. I brush his signature with my
hand for good luck and feel his sigh. He feels mine, too. I can
feel our desire move between us, spirit to spirit. I pull away
the four chairs, grab the humble tools from my backpack and
get to work. The left side is loose now, so is the top and
bottom, and most of the right; I can slide the blade along
them easily. I work my way down the final corner of the
doorframe, inserting the knife and tapping it with the
hammer, until it slides in all the way and I move lower. The
steel door is thick and I break a blade, grab another knife, and
start again. I don't bother with my penlight anymore because
I have the route of the blade memorized, my rough technique
perfected. I can feel his excitement, his joy. It matches my

own. I am trembling by the time I reach the bottom corner, loosen the last of it, and stand in front to tug it up.

It doesn't give right away, although I feel movement. I grab the oil and spray liberally around the frame, then pull and pull, over and over as he cheers me on, his anticipation growing along with mine, almost a roar in my ears now. At long last I feel the door give, swing open and upward, but only inches because it's so heavy. It clangs shut. I spray oil in the hinges along the top and pick up the old 2 x 4. Once I swing the door up, I will prop it open with the board.

Because of its weight, I have to move fast. I give a mighty yank up and the door screeches open. I attempt to stick the 2 x 4 in place before it swings back, but miss on each of the first three tries; the board falls, failing to wedge itself between the door and frame. On the fourth attempt, I succeed in bracing the 2 x 4 between the door and the frame, leaving me a wide, sturdy opening into the darkness. I'm panting and sweating even though I pulled off my jacket long ago. I slide my penlight from my pocket, turn it on, hesitate at the edge, then hear his voice.

"I've waited so long for you, Lucy…"

I've waited, too, for months, fingering his photo, tracing his figure with my fingers. I feel my body, crackling with fear and fascination, dread and desire, pushing me forward. I duck inside, straighten up, and take the first step. Surprisingly, the ground slants downward. My feet step down a dirt ramp, my penlight illuminating limestone walls glistening with moisture, and concrete over my head, the underside of the crumbling alley behind the shop. I pause, hugging my arms.

There's a wicked draft from somewhere, icier than the wind outside. It flashes to my mind I could step back and grab my jacket.

Then I see him. A brilliant light, canceling out my flashlight. It focuses into a boy my age and not much bigger, his smile beautiful, his spirit radiant. I am pulled irresistibly forward. Without thought I move toward him as he reaches his hand for me, and I reach mine for him. I have stopped breathing.

Our fingers touch. A moment of absolute bliss, and I feel my surrender. Then, without warning, electricity burns me like ice, coursing through my body, more than I can bear. I gasp and wince in pain, falling to my knees. When I open my eyes, I don't see Timothy anymore. A terrifying figure with long, dark hair and gleaming eyes looms before me in a filthy, denim shirt. I recognize him from the history book and try to scream, but can't.

"Lucy, runnnn!" Timothy screams for me. "Ruuunnn…" His voice echoes through the tunnel as I jerk my hand away and scramble for the door, crab-crawling backward up the ramp, looking with horror at the spectre before me that has engulfed Timothy. My penlight falls as I grope blindly with my hands for the opening behind me, feel the entrance as he approaches, yellow teeth grinning under glowing eyes. I hurl my body backward and feel my elbow strike the 2 x 4, knocking it loose.

The door thunders closed against my back, cutting off my escape. The heavy steel strikes my head hard, flinging me forward into the leering, monstrous remains of my long-dead abductor. He is fondling chains in his dirty fists. The door bounces once, then hits the oiled frame smoothly. The latch clicks shut.

My captor's laughter grows as Timothy's cries fade. In the absolute darkness, I feel the cold grip of shackles on my wrists as I fall to the dirt. I cry out, though I realize no one will ever hear me.

The Hut
Cathy Kern

AS I worked on catching my breath in the icy, night air, I watched my husband lean on his backpack and scan the jagged, starlit horizon above us. He spoke to Nick, pointing out the Club's ski hut amongst the mountain's shapes and shadows.

It's not that much further now," Andrew told us, his voice clear and quiet in the enveloping stillness. "The worst is behind us."

Relieved and delighted, I managed a happy little "Yay!" but Nick stood massaging his arms and didn't say a word. I got the impression he was holding a grudge from earlier.

On nights like tonight, when we arrive at the resort after the ski lifts have closed, getting to the hut means either an arduous, but beautiful, hike and climb in the dark or getting a motel and waiting till the lifts reopen in the morning. Nick, a potential new Club member on his first trip with us, had pushed for the motel. Andrew and I outvoted him; the weather was stunning and we wanted to wake up in the hut and ski straight out the door. I was surprised at Nick's sour attitude, given he was twenty-something and seemed fit.

Maybe he's tired, I thought. It *was* a particularly long drive. Or maybe he's not cut out to be a member of the Wellington Ski and Hiking Club. We'll see, I decided. None of the Club members I had checked with seemed to know much about him.

The three of us buckled on our backpacks and ski helmets, flicked on our headlamps, and started climbing again. With only cold starlight above, it was critical to focus on finding the next foothold between hidden pockets of ice-crusted snow, loose scree, and wind-swept boulders.

Suddenly, a cry from Andrew cut through the frosty air. I turned and saw him drop to his knees, tumble to his side and start sliding backwards on a patch of scree. Crouching low, I grabbed out for him—a forearm, a strap, anything; Nick did the same. The beams from our headlamps crisscrossed wildly; the crazy strobe effect lit Andrew's impact as he jolted to a stop, backpack against boulder. The two pairs of skis he was carrying in his pack's side pockets erupted onto the scree, skidded onto an icy snow patch, and picked up speed, scraping over the mountain's crusted surface as they plummeted towards the parking lot we'd left over an hour ago. Then Andrew moaned, "Claire, my back."

I was already out of my pack; I shoved it hard into a snowdrift to keep it from following our skis down the mountain. "Hang on, Honey," I responded. "Hang on." I locked my headlamp beam onto my husband and picked my way down to him, my heart in my throat. The New Zealand night sky seemed to have dropped within reach. I could hear Nick taking off and stowing his pack, too. It sounded like he was taking great care to secure his snowboard.

I was afraid, but needed to stay calm, for Andrew's sake. "Stay in the moment, Claire. Stay in the moment. Don't panic," I coached myself and then realized I'd said it out loud when

Andrew mumbled something like, "That's right."

Nick made a scoffing sound. I ignored him and tried to think.

From the pain registering on Andrew's face, I feared his fall had aggravated the same disc he'd had surgery on nine months before. I needed to make a critical choice: we could turn back and carry him for several hours over rough terrain to get him straight to a hospital, or take refuge for the night in the hut, which was in sight.

I checked my cell phone. No bars; no service. Calling for help wasn't an option.

I decided the best choice was to keep going.

I was so wrong.

Andrew passed out twice in the half hour it took us to get him to the hut. It took almost ten minutes to get him settled on the first bed inside. I felt sick with anguish.

Nick was charging around flipping every light switch he could find to no effect.

"What kind of lame ass Club cabin is this?" He fumed. "There's no power! And I'm guessing that means no heat."

"You're right about that," I said. "Can we worry about Andrew just now, though?" I started pacing around trying again to find a signal to reach 111 or mountain rescue on my cell phone.

"Look," I started, hoping to distract myself and mollify him a little. "When the Club built this hut, they installed a coal stove for heat. But some idiot burnt the cabin down in 1946, so the members decided to go with electric everything from then on." I gestured broadly at the darkness. "Sometimes it's unreliable."

I shone my headlamp around the small, open-plan cabin. The bright, but narrow beam lit half a dozen bare bunks set against the walls; two or three others, including the one Andrew was on, were still covered by wrinkled, used sheets. In the kitchen area, my beam swept across a mess of paperbacks, board games, and cereal boxes on the counter beneath the cabinets. Window curtains were left open; the weak starlight that reached inside did little to lessen the darkness in the room.

Obviously, the last group here was a bunch of selfish pigs. I tempered my anger. "There have to be compromises in a place like this. It's not for everyone."

"Yeah, well I'm getting the impression it's not for me," Nick muttered.

And I'm beginning to agree, I wanted to say, but instead told him, "Nick, it's a beautiful location. And in the morning you'll see how easy it is to just go straight out the front door, across to the lift, and go further up—if you have an annual pass—or just ski down. No lines or waiting. It's a great place."

But not for us, not this time, I added to myself, easing back down beside my husband after flicking off my headlamp so it wouldn't glare in his eyes. No matter where I walked or stood in the room, I hadn't been able to get a signal. Feeling panic starting to stir within me, I whispered to him, but he didn't answer. Even with nothing but starlight from the window over his bed, I could see Andrew was tight-lipped and sweating, despite the frigid air inside the hut.

This was bad.

Nick paced, mumbling curses and criticisms of the cabin, the Club, Andrew, and me under his breath.

Fear stoked my temper. I stood up, whirled around, and flared at Nick, "Do something useful!" The light from his headlamp shone in my eyes and I couldn't see Nick's face, but could feel his growing anger.

"I'll go out and get his pack," he snapped.

I leaned over Andrew to shield him from the blast of cold air as Nick went out and again when he returned, maybe twenty minutes later, loaded down with two backpacks—his own and Andrew's.

I glared at him. "Hey, where's mine?"

He leaned both packs against Andrew's bed and replied in a cold voice, "You're capable. Get it yourself," then squatted down and started opening Andrew's pack.

"Yes, I am. So I'll do that." I stepped close to urge him aside. He ignored me, unzipped the big top pocket, and yanked out a tightly-rolled sleeping bag I'd never seen before.

"What the... ? *Seriously?*" I gawked at him. "You had Andrew carrying your *sleeping bag?*"

Nick stood, swung his own pack across one shoulder and turned towards the empty bunks. "I'm sure he never even noticed."

"You mean you *sneaked* it in there? You didn't even *ask?*"

Nick strode across the room, the beam of his headlamp leaping ahead of him in the dark, and dumped his pack on a bed. "Who are you to talk? He was carrying your skis."

"The difference is he *knew* he was. I have asthma so he

99

offered and … he's my *husband.* You don't even *know* him."

Moving fast, he crossed back to me. "No! And if I had," he snarled, "I never would've come. What kind of idiot climbs half a mountain in the dark and plans to go backcountry skiing when he has a bad back?"

I turned my head to avoid the glare of his headlamp and shouted back, "*You* must be an idiot to think a bad back would stop my husband from doing what he loves." I stomped a step closer, we were toe-to-toe now, both still in our jackets, gloves and hats. "Andrew's surgery was successful. The surgeon *cleared* him to ski, you … *idiot!*"

"If I'm an idiot, it's for going away for a weekend with *you two,*" he growled. "I should have waited to go with a crowd of guys."

"And what? Spent your time partying?"

"Sure!" He tossed both arms in the air. "After picking up snow bunnies—the more the merrier." He'd gone from shouting to needling, which I found way nastier. "Anything in tight ski pants is fair game, preferably late teens."

"You are disgusting." I'd had enough and was about to turn back to Andrew when I saw Nick's eyebrows shoot up and his mouth drop open. His eyes were locked on something in the kitchen behind me. I turned my head to look then spun all the way around. Lit by Nick's single beam of light, I saw the cabinet doors inching open.

"What the hell…" Nick choked. I heard him take a giant step backwards. Every door came fully open then smacked shut.

SLAM! SLAM! SLAM!

I yelped and jumped back a step. Nick screamed and ran for his bunk.

"Earthquake," I thought. *"Of course."* Every year New Zealand experiences hundreds of earthquakes strong enough, or close enough to the surface, to be felt. Most people get used to the littler ones. Nick was overreacting.

But his fear was contagious. Chanting in my mind, "Stay in the moment, don't panic," I forced myself to watch and, even more so, to listen for signs this might be a larger earthquake. I turned my head from side to side, concentrating on the walls of the hut and the overhead light fixtures, straining to hear any vibrating or rattling; especially any sound like wind rushing around the exterior of the little building.

If I heard that, *then* I'd panic.

Still, standing there in the dark, in the middle of the room and kind of hunched up inside my coat, I felt really exposed. So, when the cabinet doors started edging open again, I jolted upright, right onto my tiptoes. I heard Nick run up behind me.

"Why are they doing that?" he screeched.

"I don't know!" I yelled, completely freaked out. "Shut up!"

The doors slammed fully open. *BANG!*

In a frantic dance of panic, Nick clutched at my coat, shouting and I grabbed his—both of us trying to hide behind each other and shove the other in front, our eyes locked on those cabinets—dark, gaping holes on the wall, every door standing wide open and still.

My husband moaned as if he was in pain. I knocked Nick's hands from my sleeve and ran to climb in bed next to Andrew. His eyes and lips were squeezed tight.

"Honey!" I begged in a loud whisper. He didn't respond.

Was the look on his face pain or fear ... or both? I had no idea, but I hated to hear his groaning. None of this was good. I twisted around to sit on the mattress beside him, casting a glance toward the kitchen.

There was no movement or sound.

The entire hut was silent except for Andrew's ragged breathing and his horrible, low moans. Now Nick stood in the middle of the floor, hunching into his coat and staring at the open cabinets, his headlamp sweeping back and forth.

Until a paperback lifted from the kitchen counter and hurled itself against his chest.

We both screamed. I coiled into the fetal position and scooted against Andrew, stretching first an arm and then a leg across him. I heard Nick sobbing, then, his fast, heavy footsteps as he scrambled for the door.

I raised up fast on one elbow. "You bastard!" I shouted. "You're not leaving!"

"I sure as hell am!" He jerked the door open, slammed it behind him, and was gone.

I collapsed on the bed, wanting to crawl on top of Andrew.

"Honey!" I cried, "Honey!" It was useless. He was lost in his pain, drawn inward. It was just me now with ... with what?

That was no earthquake.

Watching Andrew's pale face in the starlight, I listened with all my might, focusing behind me, too terrified to turn over and look.

"Stay in the moment, Claire. Don't panic." The mantra Andrew had taught me filled my mind. I started to cry anyway.

Flicking on my headlamp, I repeated the mantra over and over again, trying to keep the terror in my stomach from engulfing me. I slowly tore my eyes from Andrew, turned my head, and looked into the room.

My light shone on the book that had thrown itself at Nick, an innocent little bundle in the middle of the floor. The cabinets still stood open. Starlight spilled through the far windows. It was beautiful and ... peaceful. I dared, at last, to let my breath out and then I grinned. Andrew was walking his fingertips in a teasing dance along my hip and up under the hem of my jacket. Filled with relief, I turned back to him, forgetting to turn off the headlamp.

His eyes flew open. He looked right into the beam of light and giggled; the giggle of a teenage girl.

I screamed and goosebumps rose up and covered my skin. I shoved away from him, falling to the floor, and crab-walked, fast and clumsy, out of range of those insane eyes.

What the hell, I thought, *this is my husband!* I jumped up and ran at the bed. "Get out!" I screamed, "Get out of my husband! Get out! Get out!"

The giggle came again, loud and wild, from Andrew's mouth. His eyes mocked me. Behind me the cabinets slammed, books dashed against the bunk beds, game pieces scattered across the floor. I crouched, folded my hands over my head, and kept screaming at Andrew, willing him to come back.

Then I got mad. Furious.

"You're just a bully! *Stop it!* Just stop it!" I ran to the door and tore it open, still screaming. "Get out! You're not welcome here! Get out!"

Andrew went limp. Around him, the sheets lifted and tangled into a mess, threatening to pull him into the air. I leapt to the bed and grabbed handfuls of fabric, threw myself onto it, holding it down, hearing it tear, feeling something roll like waves under me, and then buck hard.

The force flung me to the floor and I felt a pressure on me. Then it was gone. Snow swept through the open door into the room. Shrieking white geysers gushed over me, rounded the room and shot back out again. The hut went silent. Shaking, I scrambled onto Andrew's bed once again, leaned on the window ledge and looked out.

All the fury was climbing the mountain above us. Plumes of snow roared uphill, growing higher and louder, merging into a wall. Stars were disappearing within it. In seconds, the sky was obliterated and still it climbed and roared.

I went cold. *Avalanche.* This thing was going to cause an avalanche.

And then I remembered.

This was not a thing. The force was a girl named Kelly. She had died in an avalanche. I'd read a tiny piece about it in the paper a year ago: a teenage snow bunny who never came home from a ski trip with friends. She was presumed dead. No details, no fanfare.

She was that wall of snow, she was livid, and she was coming back. As she surged downhill towards the hut, a wall of white about twenty feet high, roiled, aiming straight for Andrew and me.

I rushed to slam the door of the hut and took a full body blow of rage which knocked me to the wall. Doubled over, I tried to stumble to Andrew's bed. I couldn't see anything but snow, papers, blankets, sheets whirling through the hut. A child's snow globe. I heard plates smashing and windows breaking and knew we'd die.

I tried to scream over the din, choking as snow and grit filled my mouth. *"Kelly!* Stop!" I gagged and spat, fighting to bring my hands up to cover my eyes and mouth. Something hit me in the shoulder, hard. "Kelly, please! I know. I know you died."

A light fixture smashed at my feet. I struggled for breath. My chest was growing tight.

"Why are you blaming me ... us?" I cried.

A lull in the roar. I spat blood onto the snow as I tried to work out the reason for her fury. Sure, she'd died and that was terrible, but why take vengeance on us? Then it came to me. Just a teenage snow-bunny lost on the mountain..

I shouted again. This time with purpose.

"It wasn't your fault, was it? It was *his*, wasn't it? You *died* ... you died because of Nick!"

A magazine fell from near the ceiling. A blanket settled over the kitchen counter. The hut was filled with the sound of soft thuds and clattering as dozens of game pieces, utensils, and ripped paperbacks stilled in midair, then dropped to the floor.

"Thank you," I whispered, sinking to my knees. "I'm so sorry for what happened to you. I'm so sorry." The last flakes of snow spiraled down, dusting everything in white.

Shoving aside the debris under my hands, I crawled to Andrew. I cleared away twisted bedding, towels, and newspapers from his bed and found him—the real him—awake, questions in his eyes, as well as pain. I laid my cheek against his and spoke to the hut once more.

"We'll make sure people find out."

And that's what we did. While Andrew recovered from his second surgery in Wellington, I delved into the case. The night before Kelly disappeared, her friends had found her drinking with a man they all told her was too old for her. She didn't listen. The last thing she told them before she left with him was that the two of them were going off alone to ski off-piste. The man was never identified or located at the time, but her friends recognized a drawing I made of Nick.

The police would have had them identify him in a line-up, but Nick was never seen again.

I feel him, though. Every time we cross the terrain above the hut, heading to the lifts, I hear the faint sound of a teenage girl's giggle and I shiver.

Then I smile just a little.

Legend of the Sea Captain
Ric Waters

I NEVER believed in the supernatural, but I learned to my eternal sorrow that belief has nothing to do with it.

In the small seaside village of Pecatonica, New Jersey, a boardwalk lined with a variety of small shops caters to summertime tourists wanting to spend weeks basking in the sun and swimming in the saltwater.

It is the rare visitors who choose to stay overnight in Pecatonica. The majority head to Atlantic City to enjoy the sights and sounds of the gambling district and hotels up that way. Few stick around after dark. I was one of those few, having checked into a modest bed and breakfast.

Bored and having difficulty sleeping due to a preoccupation with my own petty troubles, I rose and dressed for the cooler weather that still hugged the Atlantic coast in mid-May, courtesy of easterly winds off the ocean. Tonight, however, no wind greeted me when I stepped outside.

Waves crashed against the beach, muffled and obscured by a fog I hadn't expected. It may have been 3 o'clock in the morning, but it seemed out of the ordinary that it was foggy along the shoreline.

I thought wandering along the coast and listening to the waves lapping on the sands and rocks would help calm my busy mind and set me at ease so I could return to sleep for a while before the town awoke.

Even in a community of 1,350 souls, it was inevitable that I wouldn't be the sole person out for a walk in the early morning. Why should I be the only one having trouble sleeping? Why should no one else think a visit to the ocean side would make them feel better?

Of course, I hadn't thought to bring along a flashlight, probably because I came from a much larger city where every street was lit at night by corner light poles. So, the near absolute of the darkness was a surprise. Yet, even more surprising was a sudden flickering light that appeared out of nothingness dozens of yards ahead. Probably just one of the townsfolk getting a head-start on fishing for the day, I figured.

As I continued walking, the flickering light rushed at me faster than it should have if I were simply walking toward it and its bearer toward me. As I came within range of the light, I noticed a dark figure in its faltering glow.

When the figure was close enough I ought to have been able to see it clearly, it appeared only vaguely opaque. Its shadows and colors shifted and shimmered such that at times I felt I could almost see through it. The dark figure was dressed in ratty old clothing and a knit hat, like sailors used to wear, tipped low so it covered enough of his face that I couldn't see anything distinct. The dark sailor looked and smelled wet, dripping stale, salty water that squelched underneath his boots.

I slowed my gait, more than a little apprehensive about this odd character. That was the moment I noticed the kelp clinging to his wardrobe, as if the man had been trapped in seaweed and managed to rip himself free of it before pulling himself from the ocean.

The lantern he carried in his soaked leather glove phased in and out of the fog, a small flame flickering weakly within.

Suddenly, the figure moved so quickly I barely had to time register what it was doing. Its head swung around, revealing a pale, rotting visage with a gaping wound on its cheeks and one unseeing, white eye. It opened its ghastly maw, revealing rotting and missing teeth, and lunged towards me, its free hand pointed directly at me. It made not a sound, but I yelped in surprise and found myself crashing hard against the sand and sloshing salty water.

Everything went black.

I awoke at dawn. The tide was out and the right side of my face rested on the rough, damp sand. The early light of the sun tinted the sky pink, red, salmon, and orange. The distant sounds of seagulls and the crash of waves were muffled and indistinct. My ears felt like they were stuffed with cotton.

It was only after I managed to turn my head so that I faced the sky that I noticed my vision was obscured, as if a light gray patch of cloth had been plastered over my right eye. I blinked a few times, thinking it might clear the vision, but it did nothing. I reached up to touch the eyeball and still felt a cool, firm object where my eye should be. Clearly, the eyeball was still intact, but sightless. My mind raced. What if it weren't just a temporary handicap? What if I were blind in that eye for the rest of my life?

Next, I sensed a numbness in the cheek below my sightless eye. I dragged my fingers down to touch the wet, ragged wound there. The skin was cold and clammy. I pulled my hand back and focused on it with my one good eye. No blood, which was good, but left me wondering what had happened while I was unconscious.

My hand dropped to the sand before I decided to try to get up. Even pushing myself up onto my elbows left my brain swimming, so I paused to let the feeling pass.

I managed to turn my head down far enough to see my jacket had dark splotches and strands of seaweed clinging to it. My heart jumped upon remembering the spectral figure I had seen the night before. I snatched at the kelp with one hand, pulling it off me, then fell back to the damp sand with barely a sound.

The seaweed fought my efforts to remove it from my clothing, as if it clinging to my body and intertwining itself to my coat forcefully. But, I persisted in my efforts and eventually managed to get it all off. My mind cleared somewhat once I finished the task.

I sat up all the way and surveyed the beach. A couple of people strolled at least half a mile away to the south. To the north, nothing. A few boats sat out on the water in front of me.

I shook my head, doing my best to clear the cobwebs and cotton-ear. The world gradually came back to focus, almost back to normal. Except for the grayness in that one eye.

I struggled to get to my feet and wobbled a bit, as if my legs had lost their ability to walk on land. It took a good dozen steps before it felt like I was walking like a real person. Despite the cool air, I tore off my dampened jacket and folded it, prepared to drape it over my left arm. That action brought me to a full stop.

I unfolded the fabric and held it up in front of me. It was dark brown leather, heavily weathered, showing signs of lengthy immersion in water. Yet, the jacket I'd worn out the night before had been a medium-blue, nylon baseball starter jacket.

I thought to drop the strange coat, but found that my fingers wouldn't let go. After a moment, my hands and arms turned the jacket around and shrugged me back into it without my willing them to do so. Wearing a wet coat in this weather could only lead to sickness, but, I couldn't prevent it from happening.

Then, I was stumbling back towards the bed-and-breakfast. I haltingly climbed up the three wooden stairs that led to the veranda and the front door. I threw my right hand over the right half of my face as I strode inside. Mrs. Godfrey was busy inside the dining room, serving up breakfast.

"Oh, there you are, Mr. Prentiss," she called. "Breakfast is ready, if you're hungry."

The old, matronly woman stepped into the atrium as I reached the stairway, heading for my room.

"Have you been out for a dip?" she asked.

I stopped and stiffened. "Why ... would you think that?"

"Well, your hair's all wet," she replied dourly. "And, your clothes are dripping ... all over my hardwood floor!"

"Sorry," I blurted. "I need to get to the bathroom."

I didn't wait for her to reply, simply hustling up the stairs, mindless of the rivulets of salty water falling from my slacks.

"Oh, dear!" I heard Mrs. Godfrey mutter as I rushed for my suite's door. "Such a mess!"

I located my room, pushed my way through the doorway and slammed the white board door shut, harder than I had intended to. Mrs. Godfrey yelled something up to me, but I barely heard it.

I didn't bother trying to remove the coat this time; I just trudged into the bathroom and turned on the hot-water tap with intent to splash my face and revive myself. I managed to get the water running, but didn't do anything other than stare at the ghoulish visage I saw in the mirror. My heart froze instantly and I backed away from the vanity.

In the now-fogging mirror was a pallid version of my face, ghastly altered. The big gash on my right cheek wasn't the only damage that I had suffered in my dark encounter. Several sucker-like indentations made my face look puffy and cratered, like the surface of the moon. My sightless eye was milky white; no iris, no pupil. My good eye was rimmed in red, as if I'd been crying.

Mrs. Godfrey had been right, my hair was wet and ratty, as if I'd been in the saltwater for some time. It hung in matted dreadlocks. Once I got over the initial shock, I tried to pull my hair back into some semblance of my usual haircut, but I only got a handful of gummy strands.

Steam from the hot water gradually filled the mirror. I wiped at it, but only made a big mess of it. My movements were clumsy and awkward. Water slopped everywhere.

I struggled to shut off the tap, but finally gave up and just stood there, wondering how this transformation could have taken place. I did my best to recall the night before. Everything seemed dull and insubstantial. I couldn't remember why I'd even gone out.

My arms and elbows trembled as I held myself up. I felt weak. Whatever was happening, it was getting worse.

Suddenly, I heard a shriek behind me. I turned, aghast, to see Mrs. Godfrey standing there. Towels and cleaning supplies lay scattered around her as she stared at me in horror.

"My God," she murmured. "My God!"

She backpedaled, tripping and falling spread-eagle on the pile carpeting. I quickly went to her side, grabbed her hand to help her up. She clutched it for a moment, then looked up at me and screamed again.

I stumbled back from her, taken aback by the reaction. My face. It had to be because of my face. I was scared now, too. Eventually, Mrs. Godfrey managed to get to her feet and slowly backed out of the room, pulling the door shut hard.

Despite the impairment to my ears, I could still hear her breathing hard on the other side of the door. I took hold of the doorknob and tried to turn it; it held fast, as if in the grip of someone on the other side.

"Mrs. Godfrey," I slurred, my voice suddenly changing.

"No, no, no!" she cried back.

I let go of the doorknob and stepped back. "Whatsch … whatsch … happen- … -ing?"

The innkeeper let out another short, shrill scream. A couple of other voices piped up outside. "What is it, Mrs. Godfrey?" a young woman asked.

"Are you all right?" asked a young man.

"What's going on?" asked another, indistinct voice.

"It's..." the innkeeper mumbled. "It's ... the Sea ... Sea Captain!"

The statement felt like a physical blow to me. I stumbled forward, then back, like trying to keep my feet under me in heavy waves.

"Sea Captain?" the voices whispered back and forth. "Who's the Sea Captain?"

I heard the sound of something dragged down the door. I imagined it was Mrs. Godfrey sliding down to a sitting position.

"Here, let me help you," the young woman said quietly.

A couple of minutes passed as people bustled Mrs. Godfrey away. The stairs creaked as they helped her walk down.

Finally, the doorknob turned and the door creaked slowly open. A young, shaggy-bearded man peered inside, first directly ahead of him, then towards me. He gasped and his eyes bulged as he looked upon me. "My God," he blurted softly.

When I reached out toward him, water poured off my jacket sleeve. He pulled back with a "yip."

"Do—an't—!" I slurred, my vocal cords seeming to have partially fused together and my tongue thickening.

He closed the door, the latch clicking back into place.

"What is it?" the female voice returned.

The man didn't answer immediately.

"Sam?" Her voice wavered as she spoke. "What ... *is* ... it?"

"I ... I don't know," Sam muttered. "Something's wrong. Very wrong."

I lifted my foot to step toward the door. The carpet was

soaked; it sloshed with every movement. I looked down. There was a pool of stale, black, brackish water all around me. Reflexively, I looked up toward the ceiling, but there was no sign the rapidly deepening water came from a leak. I was the source of the strange, murky puddle.

I tried to take another step and my leg seemed to lose all strength. I collapsed in the water with a splash. While I struggled to lift my torso from the floor, the door suddenly flew open. Two frightened faces stared at me. I lifted my right arm toward them, causing the woman to scream in horror. I don't know why, but I looked at my arm and saw the pallid, worm-eaten flesh on it. I was horrified by the sight, but didn't have time to make sense of it.

A force unlike anything I've ever experienced gripped me from below and dragged me into the brackish water.

"Haaaaaaallllp!" I cried as dirty, salty water filled my mouth and the thing from below pulled me under.

My worm-eaten hand was the last thing to remain above water, but my struggle was lost, so it swiftly slid beneath the surface of the water with me.

The next thing I knew, I was enveloped in dark and fog. A dim flame flickered in an aged lantern in my right hand. The waves crashed onto the shore as I strode along, seeking someone to release me from the living death into which I'd fallen.

Statuary
T S Rhodes

I ADMIT, I'm crazy. While other girls are shopping, or reading, or swiping their phones to find just the right guy, I hang out in cemeteries. I've been like this since I was a kid. My mom got a real deal on a home not far from the expansive Oak Hill Cemetery and I used the place as my playground for years. When I asked my mom about the stones, she told me that they were our neighbors. I took her at face value and memorized the names, stopping by to say "Hello!" to my favorites on a regular basis.

There was one plot that I didn't find until I was six or seven. The place was hidden by huge old trees, whose low-growing branches seemed to draw together, shielding the site from casually searching eyes. It was a large area, with space for a whole family, but only one stone marked a resting place.

Even as a child I could tell this marker was unusual. The base consisted of a square block of dark, pitted stone. Something inexpensive and local, but tall enough to come up to my chin when I had first found the place. On top of this, at eye level for me, rested a marble statue of a sleeping baby, surrounded by stone drapery and flowers. It didn't match the stone below. Even a child could see that. The two were so radically different in style, material, even purpose. The solid, square stone was a memorial. The sleeping cherub? Something else.

Most unusual of all, a peaked stone roof had been erected over the statue. Made of the same rough material as the base, it was supported by four stone cylinders, crudely shaped to resemble classical columns. The edges of the columns didn't sit evenly on the stone below. It looked like the afterthought of an afterthought.

When I was still in the early grades of elementary school, I believed this was some kind of a playhouse and the statue was a doll left by one of our "neighbors." I used to visit the place pretty regularly, mostly because of my sense there was a child here. I never saw anything out of the ordinary; only felt a certain longing about the place, as if the child in question has been sent to her room without supper.

When I grew older and learned most people were afraid of cemeteries, I stayed away for a while. I had living friends by then, and they kept me busy with Barbie dolls and cartoons. But, I'd also developed an interest in people who had been gone for decades, even centuries. So in my spare time I continued reading the memorials and following down the generations of families.

Now that I'm an adult, I love wandering past the cemetery's tributes to lives lived and lost. It's so peaceful when the twilight shadows grow long. Sometimes – not often—I get a sense of the presence of the slumbering dead. Most of them hang around just because they're too lazy and comfortable to move on. Their centuries-old sleep only adds to the tranquility of the gently rolling, wooded grounds.

The west side of the property was the earliest part used, and its stones are the oldest. The older memorials are more personal: slices of local limestone, pale and course-grained, much thinner and narrower than modern grave markers, harking back to a time when slabs were quarried by hand and hauled graveside by horse power and muscle. Their markings are different, too. Often the stones are topped by an hourglass, set there to remind the living that time is short and life fleeting.

The most interesting monuments are often so worn by wind and rain that in order to read the etched names I need to sit down beside them and do a rubbing. I tape a large piece of tracing paper over the front of the stone and carefully rub it all over with a wide hunk of artists' charcoal, so the faint, faint lines can be seen by the living.

> Come mortal Man and cast thy eye
> Read thy doom – Prepare to Die
> Ezekiel Briscombe 1746 – 1789

One summer evening I was working over an especially nice stone – spidery letters foretelling doom, topped by a folk-art flying skull, when a shadow fell over my work. I looked up to see a police officer, six foot two at least. He was chewing gum and hiding behind mirrored sunglasses, but even with these props, it was obvious that he was annoyed about something.

"Excuse me, miss. Can I help you?" His tone of voice let me know that "helping" meant picking me up and shoving me into the back of a squad car if I gave him the slightest excuse.

"Just visiting the deceased." I'd had run-ins with the police before. Crawling around on your hands and knees in a place populated by dead people draws a certain amount of attention, and I'd discovered that this was a great all-purpose answer. Besides, it was true. I just wasn't visiting MY deceased.

He glared at me suspiciously. "Well, the park's closed."

I glanced back at my rubbing. "I'm sorry, Officer. The sign at the gate said the cemetery closed at dusk." True, the shadows were getting long and bluish, and the air had cooled several degrees in the last hour, but the National Weather Service said "dusk" wouldn't happen for another twenty minutes. I had an iPhone; I had checked.

"Well that's close enough for me." He slapped his hand with a club-sized flashlight. Obviously, this was meant to intimidate me. It worked, too. But I was very close to getting my rubbing finished. I swallowed, forced a smile, and held my ground. "If you insist, Officer. I'll just finish up this up and be on my way."

Bad idea. His eyes focused for the first time on what I was doing, and he looked genuinely horrified. "You are desecrating that grave."

I glanced back at my handiwork. Paper, masking tape. (Duct tape would work better, but it leaves a residue – not good for the stone.) One crayon of soft artist's charcoal. No shovels, spray paint, or Satanic sacrifices.

I opened my mouth to explain that I was just making a

low-tech copy of the front of the stone for my own personal collection, when Officer Friendly lost his beans.

He grabbed my rubbing, crushed it into a ball, pitched it off into the growing darkness, then picked me up bodily by the collar of my shirt.

I didn't have time to do much more than yip before he dragged me to my 2002 Dodge Intrepid and threw me at the car, all the time muttering under his breath about Satanic cults and how it wasn't going to happen on his watch. Two things were pretty apparent. One, it was no use to reason with this man. Two, the sooner I got out of there the better.

My shaking hands found the keys in my pocket and I started up and drove off. Lights on, and at the legal limit of 15 miles per hour. Officer Friendly followed me in his police cruiser, with the searchlight trained right at my car, as if the Intrepid might grow bat wings and fly off into the evening shadows at any moment.

I got home at about 8:30, hungry, chilled, and still shaking. And ravenous. I didn't even need to check my refrigerator. Delivery pizza had been tonight's plan from the moment I headed to the cemetery after work, and now I desperately needed comfort food.

Only one problem. When I reached into my pocket for my phone, it was empty.

Damn. I remembered. I had taken the phone out so it wouldn't get scratched when I lay down to get at the bottom of the tombstone. Now I had no way to order pizza. Worse, there was a slim-but-remote chance that someone stopping by the cemetery tomorrow might find the phone and take it.

I began to pace. I couldn't stop by to pick it up in the morning. A cemetery keeper locked the big black-iron gates each night after dusk and took the chain off again at about 9:00 a.m. But by that time I was supposed to be sitting at the front desk at the used car dealership on the other side of town. I'm the receptionist. I'm not especially good at my job, but I am punctual.

And without the phone I couldn't even call in and tell them I'd be late.

Thunder rolled outside. Well, that did it. I was not leaving my phone out in the rain. Locked up or not, there were ways back into the cemetery, and I knew them all.

I waited a little longer, pacing nervously. Even if Officer Friendly was as hung up on Satanists as he seemed to be, there was no way he'd be wandering around on the grounds during a lightning storm. But he might be doing a regular drive-by past the street entrance.

My point-of-entrance for the cemetery would be a convenience store just south of the place. Its parking lot backed up against a line of trees and a creek which ran right past the cemetery. With a little luck (and some mosquito repellant) I would have no trouble retrieving my phone.

The scariest part of my trip was making my way around the convenience store dumpster. Some pretty sketchy characters hung out there, smoking weed and passing small objects and handfuls of cash back and forth. The dead don't bother me, but the living can be a real pain.

I was in luck. No druggies in sight. I parked the Intrepid in the convenience store lot. Clutching a dark sweater, I made my way past the dumpster and downhill towards the trickling sound of water. The rumbling thunder was still in the distance. A full moon—late rising, but very bright—helped guide me through the trees.

I kept to the north side of the creek, where there were more rocks and less mud, until I saw the old stone wall that marked the southern edge of the cemetery. Then I scrambled up the bank, scrabbling at tree roots and saplings, until I reached the wall, a low, pale construction of piled white stone.

My route gave me a good view of some markers that I hadn't paid much attention to before. Statues of men in Civil War uniform, piles of cannon balls, small artillery. A couple of mausoleums, and a strange, creepy stone statue of a tree.

And then I saw it.

It was big. About one-and-a-half life sized. A statue of a weeping woman, dressed in classical robes, the folds of the drapery heavy with despair. Her elbow rested on one knee. Her head drooped forward onto that hand, eyes closed, a few loose curls drooping free. The stone seemed as lifelike as flesh.

I'd seen hundreds of big statues like this. Some were huge, wild, over the top. Lions laying down with lambs. Flights of angels, their wings burnished with gold, or St. Michael emerging from a cloud, sword in hand.

Often times the big ones seemed overdone. As if the family is trying to make up for something. This was different. It felt *real.*

Shadows moved over the surface of the statue so that it

seemed to breathe. No, sob.

I stood, stricken, shivering in the cold breeze, watching the statue, hearing the moan of wind around the pedestal. Hair stood up on the back of my neck. A presence loomed, heavy with grief and anger. Lonely. Brooding. Powerful. I could sense it turning its attention to me, raising up, gathering itself as if it would strike me down for disturbing it, for being alive.

I backed slowly away, feeling my heart beat with fear. As if statue might come after me.

I was shivering, almost too terrified to breathe. The image over the grave seemed to be getting bigger, straining to come off the pedestal, come after me.

"Please don't hurt me," I murmured inside my head. My thoughts didn't seem to affect the rage building in the stone monster before me. It loomed over me, more frightening than the thunderstorm gathering on the horizon.

I have no idea why I said what came out of my mouth next. Maybe just desperation. But I heard my own voice croak out, "I'll fix it. I swear. I'll fix it. Just let me go."

I don't know if my promise to help had affected it, but the sense of terror and rage began to fade away. I could breathe. I stood up taller and said again, more firmly. "I want to help. I'll do anything I can. I promise."

With one more rush of sadness, the thing retreated back to its grave.

I stood for several minutes, panting. Then, because I refuse to be frightened of cemeteries, I walked (did not run) back to where I had left my phone, and picked it up just as the first drops of rain began to fall.

By the time I got back to the Intrepid, I was drenched, with creek mud up to my knees. And who should greet me when I came out into the neon light of the convenience store? None other than Officer Friendly, writing me up a ticket.

"This is private property!" I squeaked. "You can't write me a parking ticket while I'm on private property!"

His aviator glasses, reflecting the store's neon, glinted at me in malice. "The side next to the sidewalk belongs to the city. One hour limited parking." He pointed to a battered sign that no one ever paid any attention to.

I dragged my phone out into the downpour and checked the time. The car had been in the lot for 72 minutes. I cursed under my breath and took the soggy ticket with my even soggier hand.

Friendly flipped his ticket book shut with a snap. "Car like that…" he jabbed his thumb at the Intrepid, "I ought to run you in for vagrancy, too." Then with an ironic touch to his water-proof hat brim he stepped back into his squad car and drove off.

The ticket said sixty-eight dollars. No pizza for me tonight.

I ate cereal for dinner … for the rest of the week.

Saturday dawned bright and warm. I was glad of it, too. My promise to the ghost was giving me the creeps. I headed to the cemetery with a pillowcase of useful objects: camera, water bottle, tracing paper and charcoal, a yoga mat to protect me from the damp ground, and a paperback book, "First Families of the Fox River" published by the local

125

historical society. The monument's size had indicated money and, if there was any mystery about the grave's occupant, I wanted to clear it up as quickly as possible.

The towering statue, though not so impressive in daylight, wasn't hard to find. It was only stone, after all. But the same aura of sadness was there. I read the inscription.

Life's various duties to perform,
Employ'd her useful days
From lonely grief, her soul is gone,
To sing her Maker's praise.
Dolores Patricia (Gates) Hancock
Loving wife
February 10, 1822 – November 16, 1850.

Odd. No stone for a husband.

I flipped through my book, looking at names and the dates.

Here she was. Frank Garrison Hancock had been married twice, first to Dolores Gates in 1841. The marriage had been childless, and had ended with Dolores's death. Frank had then married Imogene Ann Norford and had moved away. Notes about their children—six in all. But not much more. My book was only concerned with people who had continued to live nearby.

So, Dolores had married Frank when she was nineteen, and had died childless at the age of twenty-eight. Sad enough, but not a real tragedy, at least not to me. She had just died young and her husband had moved on. Common enough.

I stubbed my toe on something in the grass. Some other,

much smaller, stones were set into the ground around her. I examined them, and that was when the horror hit.

There were twelve stones in all, each with the name of a child, each with a birth date and a date of passing that were exactly the same. Each with a full name spelled out, some with little poems or carvings of flowers. Twelve stillborn children in nine years of marriage.

I could feel the supernatural grief rise again as I imagined her going to visit the little graves, singing to them, bringing flowers, immersing herself in each tragic little death.

This was the tragedy, the reason for the huge statue, to match Dolores's massive grief.

What if she had reached what my mom called The Other Side to find no little child-spirits waiting for her? What if the little ones, in the self-caring way that children have, had moved on?

The details didn't matter. For whatever reason, there was a restless ghost here and, in some spirit of madness, or self-preservation, or whatever, I had promised to help it.

As I was walking back to the Intrepid, I saw a squad car cruising slowly down one of the cemetery's blacktopped lanes. It didn't stop, but I was careful driving out.

With no idea how to proceed, I decided on a trip to my mom's. She's a pretty grounded lady. Besides, she'd probably feed me lunch and I was still filling that sixty-eight dollar hole in my grocery budget.

Mom's original-vintage VW Beetle was at rest in her gravel driveway, and the huge shed was standing open, revealing Mom hard at work on her pottery wheel. I told my story over barbecued tofu and flax-seed cookies. Good old Mom, she never doubted me for a minute, just lit up a Marlborough and ran her hands through her hair. "So, Sweetie. Whatcha going to do about it?"

"I don't know. I've never felt anything so creepy and miserable. Most people in cemeteries are just hanging around, you know?"

Mom laughed. "If she's hanging around, she's got issues. Any way you can get those fixed?"

We talked about it a while, but short of a time machine, I couldn't figure how to put Dolores back at peace. When Mom finally went back to work in the shed—big craft fair coming up—it finally came to me, the poem on the gravestone back at my old "playhouse," the child's grave under the oaks.

This lovely bud
So young and fair
Called hence by early doom
Just came to show how sweet a flower
In Paradise can bloom

As a child, I had played at the grave for May Anne Carter because we were alike. I'd done the math. May had not been an infant when she had passed away, she had been seven.

I'd put together the family story long ago. May's parents had come to Illinois in the early 1800's. May was their only child. One hot summer day, when the TV was broken and my friends all away at summer camp, I had fallen asleep on the cool ground in front of the stone. There were no images in my dream. I simply dozed off in front of the stone, and heard a woman's voice screaming over and over, "It's raining on my baby!"

I had awakened in a cold sweat, confused. Then I'd realized in all made sense. The big, rough cube was the original memorial, ordered by May's father because her mother was too lost in grief. The later addition of the sleeping child had been the mother's tribute to her little flower. And then the miniature roof, built by a local stone-cutter, because rain fell on the image of the sleeping baby, and her mother couldn't stand to watch. I'd kept at my research long enough to learn that May's parents had fled back to Philadelphia, still childless, eight years after her death.

So the little grave was all alone. The child's spirit, which had stayed behind to comfort her weeping mother, still haunted the place. Not out of any misery of her own, but missing the woman who needed her, and who had missed her so desperately.

Too bad I couldn't get Dolores out here to babysit the little girl.

Or could I? Dolores had issues because she couldn't be a mom. May needed someone to help her make it to the next plane of existence. Was there any way I could get them together? All that lay between them was about a half-mile of curving cemetery roadway, the distance between the two graves. And of course, the fact that everyone involved was long since dead.

Well, I wasn't dead. And I had made a promise. I'd go out to the cemetery tonight, find a way to explain my plan to

Dolores, and see if I couldn't persuade her to make her ghostly way over here to visit a child who needed a mother figure.

Assuming Dolores didn't frighten me—literally—to death first.

I drove the Intrepid to the cemetery at full dark, lights out, keeping an eye out for cops, and began to make my way, on foot, between the graves.

Dolores's massive statue seemed cut into black and white shapes by the moonlight. Tonight, under a calmer sky, there was no lifelike tint to the stone, no sense of a presence. The mourning statue seemed as dead as the body beneath her.

"Hey! You!" I called up softly to the statue. "I need to talk to you!"

The statue remained mute.

My nerves pricked. "Seriously, I need to talk to you."

Nothing. She'd waited for over a hundred years. She could take her time.

I felt a strange sense of urgency plucking at me. The ghost could wait forever, but I was the one with an unfulfilled promise hanging over my head. Besides, the loneliness of little May's grave had set me on a mission. I wanted this done. I called again. Nothing. I looked around for inspiration.

The graves of the unborn children surrounded us, the little square outlines of the stones easier to pick out in the moonlight. Several had wildflowers growing near them; others were obscured by weeds. On impulse, I reached down a plucked a flower.

A restless vibration from the big statue.

I moved to another grave, plucking another flower. A cold shiver went down my back. I moved to the next grave. This time when I bent over a cold breeze slithered down my back. I spoke to the cold. "Dolores … Look, your children have moved on. They don't need you anymore."

A sudden, enormous wind rose, knocking me down and pinning me to the damp earth. I chanced a look back at the statue. It shimmered, exuding rage and pain. The ghost wailed.

"Dolores … I came here for your help." What I really wanted to do was get out of there, to run right out of the cemetery. But the cold and my own fear held me paralyzed. It felt as if every organ in my body was going into deep freeze.

A mass of anger settled over me, until I could hardly breathe. The cold was sinking in toward my core, making me tremble in every limb. Desperately I gasped out into the darkness. "There's a little girl, Dolores. She's alone, like you. She needs a mother."

Something else. A question, maybe.

I could breathe a little better, at least. I gasped and sat up on the grass and told the hovering spirit everything – May's family, her distraught mother, how her dad had taken his wife away so she wouldn't obsess over the grave any more.

"So you see," I concluded, "She needs a mother figure in her life … her death. Her parents are on The Other Side by now, but she needs help passing over, so she can find them. And, you know…" I swallowed. This was dangerous ground. "Your kids might be over there. You could see them again."

The hovering presence softened. Carefully, I climbed to

my feet. "Can you come with me? You'll have to come to the opposite side of the cemetery."

I sensed her move toward me, but then the sensation of movement halted suddenly at the row of stones for her children, as if blocked by some invisible force.

I thought for a few moments, then did the only thing I could think of; I tended to the graves of her forgotten babies. I pulled the weeds crowding some of the small square memorials and gathered a few nearby wildflowers, laying one on each grave, making sure Dolores or whatever was holding her back knew that someone else shared in her grief.

I turned and started walking. Slowly, carefully. As if I was walking on egg shells. Or through a field of land mines. Behind me, the presence hovered, doubtful, perhaps ready to attack, but finally I felt her move beside me, past the stones, but still chilly, uncertain.

And dead. Definitely dead. I had never minded cemeteries, but strolling through a cemetery next to a dead person really choked me with fear. I kept a steady pace down the paved lane toward the far side.

We were nearly there when I heard the siren behind me and saw the flashers. Cop car. Officer Friendly, for sure. He'd snagged the caretaker's key just so he could snag me. I stopped in my tracks, feeling the presence beside me expand and grow colder.

"Well, what have we got here?" His bulky form came into view, pulling out his ticket pad. "I'm thinking criminal trespass, vandalizing a cemetery, desecration of a grave, or graves…"

"Officer," I said, my stomach tensing up, the hair on the back of my head standing on end. "I know I'm not supposed to be here after dark, but there was kind of an emergency…" Beside me, the ghost stirred. The hair on my arms stood up. I could almost hear Dolores growl.

"I.D., please," Officer Friendly went on, without even looking up from his pad.

My numb fingers fumbled in my jeans pocket for my wallet. I held it out.

The air beside me became Antarctic cold. "Come on! I don't have all night." Friendly had his huge flashlight out, lit, and was thumping it in his hand like a club.

I stretched out my arm, holding my driver's license closer. "It … It's right in my hand."

"Both of you."

He could see the ghost? I hadn't seen her. I had only felt her presence and her increasing rage. I chanced a quick glance and saw her, myself, but could also see nearby gravestones through her ghostly image. Officer Friendly seemed oblivious to Dolores' semi-corporeal state, not even noticing when a flick of his flashlight shined a beam right through her. So much for the vaunted observational skills of police officers.

"Fine" the cop snarled. "No I.D.? Then it's handcuffs and the back of the squad car for you both." He stuffed his pad in his pocket and grabbed his cuffs from his belt with his other hand, moving past me, toward her. "You first." He nodded in my direction. "I know where *she* lives."

He reached out for her…

I heard one sound … A sort of squeak. The cop's face went dead white. Whiter than a human face ought to go. I watched in horror as every hair on his head stood on end. And then he just keeled over sideways. I stared down. He was on his side, stiff as a board, looking like a mannequin that's been pushed over. He was breathing. I saw that. Then Dolores moaned beside me.

I started walking again, double-time.

When we reached the far side of the cemetery, I led the grieving mother through the trees to the little statue. The chill in the air drifted away. Instead, for the first time, I felt warmth coming from Dolores.

I felt May's presence under the trees.

There was nothing to see, really. The dappled moonlight stayed the same. But the feeling of sadness that had always hovered near the little girl's resting place began to fade away. And after a while, I thought I heard a woman singing, and the soft laughter of a child.

Irene
Melanie Waghorne

IRENE WASN'T particularly religious, but ever since she had been a young girl she had heard the voices of the dead. They clamoured at the edges of her peripheral vision, pulled on her hands, sobbed and begged for her help. Their thoughts would come to her unbidden during a moment of reflection, a brief lull in normal conversation, and in the nether-world between awake and dream. The spirits perched on the edge of her bed, the edge of the bath, the edge of her seat, the edge of her consciousness, and told her about their regrets, the things they hadn't done, the things they wished they could say.

She felt their memories as if they were her own—a last embrace at the hospice, a late night phone call about a tragic accident, the tone of a flat line on a hospital monitor, the feel of a cold gun at her temple. She wept in the depths and chasms of other people's memories, gathering them up like fishing nets, pulling them back, feeling the remembrances like barbs tearing through synapse, nerve, and muscle. She absorbed their stories and relived their sorrows in her dreams, until she woke keening.

Irene began to feel like a ghost herself, with no space for a life of her own, crowded out by the lives of the dead. She was constantly hounded by their presence, constantly choking back tears that she didn't know belonged to her or a stranger. She didn't know what to do.

And then she did.

She sat at the bus stop one morning and thought about how she would do it, how she would join their ranks. She wasn't too far from the coast; she could drown herself. But she abhorred the thought of not knowing where she would end up, washed up one morning fish-nibbled and naked for a morning jogger to stumble over. She needed something a bit more intimate and much more clothed. At home, so only a policeman would find her when the smell started to bother the neighbours. Yes, that would do nicely.

She was so caught up in her plans, she hadn't noticed the spectre sit between herself and another young woman waiting with her on the bench.

"She was going to be my wife," the spectre mused. "That girl there. She didn't know yet, mind, but I had it all planned out. I had the ring bought and everything."

Irene sighed; closing her eyes did not block out the sound of his narrative.

"I'd put it in the inside pocket of my best suit, all pressed and hanging in my wardrobe for that night, so I wouldn't lose it. I booked a table at a nice restaurant and I went to work. I was in such a rush on my way home on the bike to get dressed, I didn't see him turning."

"Stop it" Irene whispered. The lady next to her flicked her a look.

"Didn't see him turning and then BANG!" He clapped his hands together and Irene jumped. "Right into his bonnet. All over his bonnet, in fact, but all I could think of was that ring sitting in my jacket pocket at home."

Irene began to cry.

"Did you hear me? It's in my bloody jacket pocket, just sitting there in the wardrobe and she hasn't bloody found it! Look at me! Look at what became of my plans, my dreams!" The young man turned his head towards Irene, revealing his caved in skull, his eye viscous and bulging.

"Stop it! Stop it! Why can't you leave me alone? Why is this my problem?" She stood up and turned to the startled woman next to her. "He wants you to know that it's in his jacket pocket, the inside one, in his best suit hanging in the wardrobe. Oh, and he was a bloody idiot for driving so fast."

She barely managed to register the look of agonized shock on the woman's face before she began to run. She just wanted to outrun their pain and be alone with her own.

Irene made it back to her flat, sweaty and resolved. She had no one in her life that she needed to make peace with; no friends, no close co-workers. Her ever-oblivious parents were sunning themselves as ex-pats in the Costa-del-Wherever, phoning only once every couple of months. She wouldn't leave a note; she would just do it, tonight she would finally find some silence. The thought of infinite silence made her smile, released a weight inside her chest.

She marched into her bathroom and opened the medicine cabinet. She carried the bottles through to the bedroom in her arms and dumped everything out on the duvet, scattering them like confetti. She didn't have a lot, some Tramadol left over from a tweaked back, Ibuprofen, Paracetamol, Feminax, Vitamin C, but she planned to use it all. She wanted to be sure.

Irene looked at the pills, spread like fallen petals on the bed, and decided they might not be enough without alcohol. She proceeded to get sloppily, mournfully drunk, not bothering to put on the light as the evening sank into night. Around midnight, she felt the mattress give as someone perched beside her. She turned to the familiar biker, who was looking at her with the good side of his face.

"Oh Christ, really?" she shouted. "Couldn't you even have the decency to let me kill myself alone? You're all bloody voyeurs!" Next doors' neighbors banged on the wall.

The young man placed his hand over hers, the sensation was cold, an icy mist.

"She found it you know. Because of you, she decided to have a look, she went back to our house and she found the ring. I watched her pull it out and put it on. She was crying, but in the end she smiled, after cursing me a bit, well, a lot, actually" The ghost coughed out a laugh. "I hope she knows how much I really loved her, even if sometimes I was a bloody idiot like you said. That was thanks to you that was. If you didn't go all raving loony out there, that suit and that ring might have ended up in the charity shop and she might only have thought of me as that idiot who left her with no goodbye and a crumpled motorbike."

Irene looked up at his road-ravaged face.

"I'm trying to say thank you."

She glared at him through involuntary tears.

He gestured to the pills strewn over the bed. "They won't leave you alone if you're dead, you know. You'll have to hear their stories all the time. Imagine being in a doctor's waiting room for eternity with the whiniest old codgers you could find with no sense of personal space." Irene snorted a little laugh through her tears. "That's what it's like, a bad case of terminal regret."

He patted her hand once more and was gone.

Irene awoke the next morning, shaky and sick from her hangover. The dead were always full of regret, but she had actually helped one of them. She wanted to try to help some of the others, not just be passively bombarded by their burdens. She wanted to alleviate some of their anguish, move them along, at least out of her life.

That's when she saw the job advertised at Forest Lane Funeral Home and Crematorium. They were looking for a new technician to handle the cremations. A lonely job, to be sure, but helpful for her purposes.

At Forest Lane, she could spend most of her day away from the living. It made the dead seem less deafening. She had always found working in offices too loud, both the living and the expired fighting for her attention. If she let her concentration drop, she would accidentally mix the two worlds, answering the questions of the dead aloud or confusing their stories with those of her co-workers. Suffice to say, she was not very popular in the office, but you couldn't sack someone for being a bit weird. Forest Lane was different; she enjoyed opening the chapel first thing in the morning. She would often sit in one of the pews and run her hand along the smooth lustre of the wood, feeling the condensation of thought, as light and saturating as summer rain.

In the warm belly of the cremation room, Irene could give her full attention to the spirits who came to her. Most often they were those whose coffins she was handling. She would listen to their stories, then ask them if there was anything that she could do. Sometimes they just wanted to talk and Irene would settle herself at her workbench, hands clasped around her mug and listen. Sometimes they asked her to visit their stones later on. They wanted to know that they would not be forgotten, that someone would be there to care if their graves grew wild with climbers or moss. Irene became a regular at the cemetery. So much so that the groundsmen knew her by name and tended to the stones if she couldn't.

At home, Irene adopted an elderly one-eyed tabby cat that a ghost had implored her to take in. Her name was Emily, the ghost had said. "I've had her since a kitten, she won't know what to do in a shelter."

That had been a welcome request, some living company. However, sometimes the requests were too hard—relatives across the world, precise location or new name unknown. Sometimes the spirits who confided in her just didn't want to be dead; they wanted to hold their child, kiss their lover, see the world. Sometimes Irene couldn't help them, but she would cry with them.

From time to time, a ghost came to her and, like the biker at the bus stop, asked her to pass on a message. If she was lucky, it was to one of the mourners upstairs in the chapel. After the service, she would slip quietly into the crowd of well-wishers, take someone aside, and pass on the message from the spirit. It didn't always go well. Sometimes the loved one would refuse to listen, thinking her sick or mad.

Once she was even accused of being a mistress. After all,

how could she possibly know all of this information about someone's deceased husband if she'd never met him before?

She recited one message only to find out with a resounding slap that it was the ghost's last passive-aggressive dig in what had been an already tumultuous marriage.

Sometimes it wasn't just the mourners who were angry; the ghosts would blame her for bad reactions, for not giving the message quite right. On those days Irene would go home with a headache after a day of scolding and berating.

Irene passed on messages and carried out errands for months, until her life was full of duties for the expired. She was tired. It was obvious that the deceased were talking her up, recommending her on some other world Yelp!. More often than not her conversations with them started with "I heard," "I was told," "There's a rumour that…" and so forth. Soon her one-on-one conversations in the warmth of the crematorium basement turned into shouting matches, as an assembly of spooks jostled for her attention.

Not just at work, they shouted when she ate her breakfast, when she bathed, as she used the toilet, even nudging her awake from sleep to tell her to weed the stones, pen a poison letter to the new boyfriend, tell him/her/it that they loved/missed/revered/hated them. It was exhausting. She was exhausted.

Irene began to nod off at all times of the day. Her head would begin to sag as she sat at her workbench, against the tiled wall in the shower, and just before her car hit the crash barrier.

Her eyes flicked open in sudden terror as the front of the car crunched through the steel guardrail, slamming the steering

141

column into her stomach, doubling her over like a rag doll. Her head smashed into the windscreen, leaving a mark like a spider's web. The car forged through the heavy barrier, to the edge of the bridge. She felt a sickening lurch in the pit of her stomach as it teetered, front wheels rolling desperately in thin air, and fell. The world was only pain and a kaleidoscope of air, water, and glove-box detritus before the car hit the river, hard as if it were concrete.

Frigid water rushed through cracks in the doors, windows, and windscreen, soaking Irene and wakening her to even greater pain. She gasped and gulped at the water, heavy with the taste of minerals. The car bobbed a little under the weight of water and foundered. Irene took a gulp of air before the water went over her head and the car submerged, bumping itself along the riverbed. Irene's hair rose like tendrils of seaweed in the tide, her blood blooming, swirling, and dancing in the current. She tried pulling at the doors, but they held tight with burden of the water. The last of the air burned in her chest and her vision began to darken at the edges.

A hand curled cold fingers around her wrist. In the murky water floated a pale face, not one of rescue, but bloated and decayed, skin floating from the skull like a wedding veil. Words bubbled up from its mouth, "I heard you can help me." Beyond it floated many more, faces of the drowned snared among the riverweeds. The last of the trapped and searing air left her in a panic of bubbles and a muffled scream, allowing the river to surge into its place.

Cold-Nosed and Cold-Hearted
Jean Rabe

SUE'D BEEN cold-nosed in her living years, so she was the first to notice the tracks. Mebbe they was pressed so lightly in the earth that a bug wouldn't give 'em no nevermind, but Sue could follow 'em.

And whatever made these tracks was festering in her craw. I could tell 'cause Sue had her scruffy hackles up and tail swinging low.

She growled so soft it seemed a suggestion o' a sound.

They couldn't've been connected to no big official happening, 'em tracks ... not left from men holding a sanctioned burial or attending some whoop-de-do with songs and a picnic and a photographer taking pictures and directing folks where to stand. I would've felt the weight o' that many tramping around, and the music would've skittered down through the dirt and disturbed my rest. I would've heard all o' the voices.

Not left by T-Bone Williams either; I always felt him when he came traipsing up here to tend the graves. T-Bone, he courted three hundred and fifty pounds if he went an ounce. The dirt seemed to protest his walking on it. But Sue wouldn't've been bothered by T-Bone's tracks.

Mebbe they was the tracks o' a critter or a nosey trespasser; mebbe from someone leaving flowers. But I didn't see no new flowers when I drifted up after the sun went down … just some withered daisies tied with a hank o' pink ribbon that Old Man Shrader'd set out for Peaches a handful o' days past. The stars so bright and sky so clear I could see that the petals on 'em daisies was all curled and the shade o' brown hen's eggs, probably starting to stink. Old Man Shrader'd been coming here every other week since Peaches died. He'd set out flowers or biscuits or sometimes an old ball next to the headstone, tap the top o' the marker, and mumble a prayer. The years were overtaking Shrader now, and maybe on one o' his daisy bringing trips he wouldn't have the strength to shuffle back down the hill.

That'd suit me just fine. I've been craving human company. Even mumbling Old Man Shrader'd do. Some dead soul to jaw with.

All o' a sudden, Sue bayed, the note long and low and mingling with the melodies o' the peepers down in the bog and the hoots o' the big barred owl perched overhead in the crook o' my tree. I enjoyed all the night music and rested my transparent backside against the trunk to listen and to watch what Sue was up to.

A mist was forming, and Sue stuck her nose down into it. The fog was settling thick and quick 'cause the air was chilling this October night, the ground still warm from the day's sun. The mist made the place downright spooky, and it flowed up to her hocks like it was hugging her.

Sue raised her head and bayed again and again, summoning the lot o' 'em. They rose with the fog, 'em dead doggies, wispy tail tendrils curling around the headstones and trees, their

144

ghosty bodies emerging through the sprawling patches o' shoulder-high pampas grass. Dozens o' 'em. Mebbe a hundred, mebbe all two hundred, was in the pack tonight.

I knew some by name: Sue o' course, she always came out first. Peaches, Preacher, Patches, Purple ... lots o' 'em starting with the letter "P." Smoky the bluetick, Bean Blossom, Duncan, Buddy, Lady, Amos, High Pocket, and Happy Higgins the Plotty. And Troop, o' course. He was usually the last to come out, and on many nights he never bothered. He was the biggest o' 'em all, the tallest, had the widest withers, and the longest snout.

Troop floated through the others and went shoulder-to-shoulder with Sue, his wispy muzzle pointed straight ahead, dead eyes fixed on something far beyond this piece o' 'Bama soil. He bayed along with her, so mournful a noise I'd never heard before dying. Troop's throaty sound had a way o' pulling in all the sadness in the world and sending it back out like a thousand women was wailing for men never coming home from war.

Troop'd been the start o' it, the first coon dog buried here. He'd lived nigh onto sixteen summers, two more than nature usually permitted according to Kipling's poem, and his man had buried him deep in the meadow at the crest o' this hill. The spot'd been a camp, and hunters'd gathered at it to smoke and chew, brag up their coonhounds, and tell stories that most o' which weren't true. I heard all o' their chatter through all o' the years drifting down through the dirt and settling around my bones. Some o' 'em tales—probably the only honest ones— had been about Troop. None o' 'em hunters disputed that he'd

145

been the best, and they'd all hung their heads respectfully when that dog was mentioned. Folks still hold that doggie's name in reverence today.

Troop started pacing, and I could tell he was tense. Usually nothing bothered that old ghost dog, and so I was curious. He shared some whimpered conversation with Sue, punctuated by snorts and pawing at the mist-covered ground, followed by a wuffling not unlike a horse could make. In all my decades in the dirt, I'd never been able to decipher dog-speak. But I know it's a language, a complex and secret one.

Troop was planted here on the fourth o' September o' '37, wrapped in a sack, name chiseled on a rock—royal treatment compared to what I got a hundred years before. He was the first dog buried here, but others came after, the hunters deciding it the perfect spot for their deceased best friends. About two hundred are planted here now, all coonhounds o' some stripe, all with markers o' some kind to note their passing—crude wooden crosses and planks, to plaques o' hammered sheet metal, to engraved marble slabs that must've cost hundreds o' dollars and took a considerable effort to lug up this ways.

"A Good Dog."

"A Joy to Hunt With."

"Not the Best, But the Best I Ever Had."

"Rest in Peace."

The only cemetery o' its kind in the world, so they say. A tourist attraction that draws folks from all over to this little corner in northwest 'Bama, the footfalls from their whoop-de-dos wriggling down to pester what's left o' my bones. I've heard a loud woman during September shindigs hawking T-shirts to commemorate the visit to this sacred spot. Sometimes she also hawked caps ... making money off dead doggies. It ain't right.

I wonder if 'em ghost hounds realize how much o' a to-do is made about 'em.

I'm the only man planted here, and those what put me in the ground are long ago ashes, probably all nice and buried somewhere proper with stones that say who they was—but not what awful deed they done. I hope they're rotting in hell.

Troop turned his head, hollow eyes staring my way, eating into my soul. If I'd been breathing, that look would've given me the willies. As it was, the damn dead dog still unsettled my spirit and pinned me in place like I was some fat raccoon he'd just treed.

The hunters all said Troop was cold-nosed, mebbe because he was a redbone, that he could follow tracks until they came fresh and would keep something in a tree until a hunter shot it down. Mebbe all redbones are cold-nosed. Sue'd been a redbone when she was breathing. Now she was just bones.

Lots o' bones in this stretch o' ground, all cold.

Troop looked away and I relaxed.

I'd wager that indeed all two hundred was up tonight, Sue and Troop a coaxing 'em from their slumber. The individual bodies was difficult to discern, as they faded in and out and moved through each other. Most kept their feet well into the mist, but a few rose above it ... eerie.

I watched Sue, she always led the pack. Always. I wondered why Troop let her.

They quieted, and she inched forward, into a stand o' tall pampas, not disturbing a single blade. The night so still, the grass didn't shush together and the leaves overhead didn't rustle. If it weren't for the frogs and the owl, it'd be right disconcerting. Troop followed her after a moment, and then the others, folding in on each other and spilling down the side o' the hill like a stream o' smoke puffed from a big-bowled pipe. I laid out flat and ghosted above 'em. They stopped after a handful o' minutes, and I eased to the front, seeing Sue stick her nose deep into the mist again. Following something, definitely.

She bayed, and Troop's mournful howl drowned out her voice, then the others started snorting and pawing, making wuffling sounds, the dead chorus drowning out the peepers' song. I imagined that the racket was so loud it would've been painful, but I was well more'n a hundred years past feeling pain. I'd lived in a cabin near a big spring in the foothills o' the Appalachian Mountains, and I went often into Tuscumbia. The steamboats that stopped at the landing is why my bones are in this hill. I'd taken to conning some o' the fancy-looking passengers. One night I ran afoul o' some folks more ill-tempered than me and they trussed me up in the back o' a wagon and took me out here, drug me up the hill and hung me. I remember 'em laughing, and one fellow who was a grinagog spat at me as I breathed my last. Cursed me, he did. I think that curse kept me from seeing what was on the other side o' death, and kept me close to this tree. I can't drift more'n a few miles from it. But 'em dead doggies can, damn 'em all.

I worried that whatever Sue and Troop was tracking was

mebbe beyond my ghosting limit. I wanted to see what had 'em all so bothered. Their baying came louder still and they flowed faster, and I could barely make 'em out, the fog thick, the dogs so numerous, it all looked like feet-deep cotton.

I felt the tether to my tree pulling tight and knew I couldn't go much farther. Just then Troop reared above the others, his baleful keening bah-rooooo rising higher than everything and encouraging the massive pack to join in the baying. I knew then for certain that the living couldn't hear the dead. There were little cabins in the hollers, and the piercing cacophony would've rattled all the windows and doors and pulled the folks out to see the hunt.

That's what this was—a hunt, and at the edge o' my vision I spied the quarry. Two black bears. One was big, more than three feet high at the shoulders and might've gone double T-Bone's weight. The other was roughly half that size and was halfway up a tree, intent on a boy straddling a thick branch. Didn't matter to me whether Sue'd been tracking the boy or the bears.

The boy had a canvas sack over his shoulder, mebbe something tasty in it that caught the bears' attention. 'Bama always had a considerable black bear population, and they usually let people alone. But all the homes springing up, towns spreading out … bears gotta eat, I figure.

The bears paid 'em dead doggies no nevermind. Couldn't hear 'em, couldn't see 'em. I wondered why Troop and Sue and all o' the others just didn't let the bears be and let nature take its course. The boy would either climb higher and the bears would lose interest, or the boy would be bear food. I was hoping the bears would win; I thought it might be interesting to see a youngster pulled apart and devoured.

Troop raced forward, taking the lead from Sue. I watched him nip at the big bear's haunches. I would've laughed at how ineffective that was, but ain't nobody would've heard me. Sue joined him, and Purple, Bean Bottom, Duncan, and Happy Higgins the Plotty followed. A moment more and all o' the two hundred had swarmed the big bear, some o' 'em doggies floating up the trunk and snapping at the smaller one.

In all my years under the ground I hadn't known the dead could harm the living. But this old dog learned a new trick. I watched 'em pass through the bears over and over and over again, and I saw 'em bears shudder like they was freezing. The little one scampered down the tree and dashed for the thick part o' the forest, but the big bear stayed intent on his prize, rearing back and snarling, setting his front claws against the trunk. I could see him try to shake off the cold 'em doggies was bringing him, ruff all thick and raised, mouth wide and glistening all hungry and angry.

Troop's howls mingled with the bear's growls. What, with all the yips, baying, and barking, it was an awful tumult. The noise was like a solid thing, a palpable smothering presence. The pack melded and melted into the bear and frost formed thick on its hide, icicles grew from its mouth, and its black eyes glazed over. The great beast shook once and released its hold on the tree, then fell dead.

The pack flowed out o' the corpse and away from the tree, slipped into the fog and lost itself in the high pampas grass. I could still hear 'em, though, snorting and yowling softly in their complex secret language.

I watched the boy now. He climbed down the tree, eyes wide. Had he seen 'em doggies somehow? Or was he merely in shock? I put him at about twelve, mebbe thirteen, certainly no older. He clutched his canvas sack to his chest with one arm, and with his free hand oh-so-tentatively touched the bear. His breath puffed away from his face in a lacy fan, like it was winter rather than early October.

I figured he would've ran away, farther than my tether allowed, the night's activities done, and him scared. But he didn't. He stared at the pampas patch, then looked up the hill, wiped a tear away from his eye, and started up. I flowed above him, curious.

Sue and Troop padded behind him, the rest o' the pack a cloud that spread away, almost indistinguishable from the mist. At the top o' the hill, the boy took in the cemetery.

I realized what was in the sack. But, it wasn't big enough to be a coonhound.

This cemetery was exclusive. Only coonhounds. No shepherds or retrievers or lapdogs or—God forbid—a poodle or some froo froo little yappy thing was allowed. There's rules for planting a dog here. The owner and a witness has to declare the dog a genuine coonhound, and a member of the Coon Dog Memorial Graveyard, Inc.—note they got all legalized with that "Inc."—has to view the body and also declare it as such. All o' it sanctioned by 'Bama's State Lands Division to allow for the graves, as the ground is state soil.

The boy found an empty spot not far from Troop's grave and pulled a small spade from his back pocket. It took him a long while to dig the hole, the ground being hard, and him crying and stopping to touch the sack, to open it and pet the dead dog inside. An old small dog, black, but with a white muzzle; some sort o' mutt that the society would've poo-pooed. The boy kissed its head, then put it in the grave, reverently covered it and tamped it all down. Clever boy, he spread rocks and brush over it so mebbe T-Bone wouldn't notice when he came to maintain the headstones.

Troop and Sue watched the proceedings. The rest o' the pack had either lost interest and went elsewhere or, out o' respect, simply disappeared.

The boy sat there for another hour, touching the dirt, finally saying something. His dog's name had been Penny, and he said he would miss her and would come every day, bring her some flowers. I 'spected the pack would accept her, doggies not being so particular as men. I 'spected Penny might rise tomorrow night and howl with Peaches and all o' the others.

Sue and Troop left.

'Em dogs were cold-nosed, 'em two.

I glided closer.

I was pretty sure 'em doggies couldn't do anything to me; I was beyond this world and beyond pain, a spectre like 'em and yet different 'cause I didn't know their secret tongue. Still, I waited until they were gone … just in case. Then I used the trick they'd taught me tonight. I flowed into the boy and stayed there, making him so cold, frost formed on his fingers and his tears froze on his dirty cheeks. I stayed and held so tight to him he seized and twitched and finally fell down upon Penny's grave.

Sue and Troop was cold-nosed.

I was cold-hearted.

I stayed until I felt the boy's soul slip into the ground, then I followed it and grabbed onto it so tight I knew it would never leave this plot in 'Bama.

I finally had me some company that I could talk to.

I 'spect we'll chat first about dead dogs.

Author's Note: *The Coon Dog Cemetery is located seven miles west of Tuscumbia, Alabama, on US Hwy 72. Commemorative caps, pins, and T-shirts can be ordered via the website: coondogcemetery.com.*

The Editor and Authors kindly ask you to please consider
writing an honest, thoughtful review of this publication.

Author Biographies

Donald J. Bingle is the author of a variety of books and about fifty short stories in the horror, mystery, thriller, science fiction, fantasy, steampunk, romance, comedy, and memoir genres. His company, 54-40' Orphyte, Inc. has already produced a variety of game and publishing products, including his series of Writer on Demand story collections. In addition, with more than a decade as a speaker and panelist for the GenCon Writers' Symposium and a member of the St. Charles Writers' Group, he has vast experience in editing and critiquing stories in a wide variety of genres. Visit his website: donaldjbingle.com.

Sarah Hans is an award-winning editor, author, and teacher. Her short stories have appeared in about a dozen publications, but she's best known for her multicultural steampunk anthology, *Steampunk World*, which appeared on io9, Boing Boing, Entertainment Weekly Online, and Humble Bundle. The anthology also won the 2015 Steampunk Chronicle Reader's Choice Award for Best Fiction. You can find Sarah floating in the aether above Columbus, Ohio or online at: sarahhans.com.

Dolores Whitt Becker was born and raised in Wisconsin and settled in Batavia, Illinois after a couple of decades of more or less aimless wandering. In addition to writing, she has been a music student, an artists' model and an actor, while occasionally holding a real job too dull to mention. When she was hired by the public library, she finally knew what she wanted to be when she grew up. She was thirty-four at the time. She has been married and divorced, had two children and lost one of them. Her first professional sale was to the first issue of *Mountainland Magazine*, which folded shortly thereafter; however, a copy can be checked out from the Batavia Public Library. She is currently a member of the Fox Valley Writers Group, which publishes an annual anthology entitled *Fox Tales*.

William Pack got his first job in a magic shop at the age of 11 and he has been perfecting his trade ever since. He is a graduate of the Chavez College of Manual Dexterity and Prestidigitation, an award winning professional magician and storyteller, Victorian séance reenactor, former card cheat, ex-casino surveillance, occasional author, world-renowned magic historian, and magic consultant for the movie *Ali*, starring Will Smith. The legends of his Great Aunt Bernice and the ghosts he inherited from her have appeared in his modern day spook shows, Familiar Spirits, The Haunting, and City of Ghosts. Further information on William can be found at: williampack.com.

Lynne Handy is a member of the St. Charles Writers Group, Fox Valley Writers Group, Chicago Writer's Association, Kentucky State Poetry Society, and Sisters in Crime. In 2013, she self-published a novel, *In the Time of Peacocks*, and her work has been published in *Clementine Poetry Journal*, *Memoir Journal*, *Lark's Fiction Magazine*, and *Pegasus*. A retired library director, she lives in North Aurora, Illinois, where she enjoys nature, and writes poems and short stories. Visit her website: lynnehandy.com.

Wren Roberts named herself and ran away from home at fifteen to pursue writing and filmmaking. Her written work has previously been featured in *The Interlochen Review, The Minetta Review,* and on off-off-Broadway. She once won a reality show and views that as one of the stranger things that's happened. She currently lives with three naughty kittens and a naughty Russian outside Chicago. She can be found on twitter as @gardsmyg or at her website: wrenroberts.com.

Kate Johnson combines humor, feeling, and misadventure in her work, pulling it together with quirky characters who don't or won't fit into their world. She's written three novels she's in the process of publishing: the young adult romance, *Aly & Abe;* the family comedy, *Learning to Read;* and the murder-mystery, *Skip Tracer, Heart Breaker.* "The New Girl" is based on her experiences long ago working in an old photo shop. Her own ending, thankfully, was less spectacular. This is her first published ghost story; she scared her pants off writing it. She lives in St. Charles with her long-suffering husband and their three clever teen-agers, barking dogs, and beleaguered cat. Reach her at: katj09@comcast.net.

Cathy Kern fell asleep as a child listening to the distant sounds of trucks passing through Illinois summer nights. Wanderlust and imagining other people's stories took hold and have shaped her life since. With thirty years of writing experience, Cathy has been published in the U.S., New Zealand, and Australia. She has written award-winning copy for clients such as McDonald's and MasterCard, non-fiction essays for national and community magazines, and website content for clients ranging from a Vietnamese orphanage to a horse ranch. She took part in New

Zealand National Radio's production of her love poem set in the 1000 Acre Wood, is thrilled by the existence of leafy seadragons, and fascinated by the conversations of strangers. Cathy would now rather write than sleep. She can be reached at: cathy@kernbetts.com. Her first novel, *My View of the Bright Moon*, is due out in 2016.

Ric Waters is a writer and photographer based in Aurora, Illinois. He is the author of "Out of the Darkness," a short science-fiction story which appeared in *Foxtales 3*, an anthology by members of the Fox Valley Writers Group. The cover art of the same publication is a photo Ric took. Ric's writings are primarily science fiction, historical fiction, and suspense. He has penned a short series of novellas based on the fictional sci-fi program "Inspector Spacetime," available for reading at btvbooks.wordpress.com. A couple of his flash-fiction stories may be found at: fewerthan500.com.

TS Rhodes spends some of her time haunting cemeteries, and has seen both of the graves mentioned in her story. She is one of the web's foremost experts on pirates, writing *The Pirate Empire* blog at: thepirateempire.blogspot.com, as well as authoring the historically accurate, but fictional series of books also called *The Pirate Empire*, including *Scarlet Sails, Bloody Seas, Gentlemen and Fortune*, and *Storm Season*.

Melanie Waghorne is a twenty-nine year old author living in Gravesend, UK with her fiancé and Ripley the dog, an animal much shyer than her alien exterminating name-sake! She is a writer with a caustic sense of humour, twisted imagination, and a portfolio of paranormal, ghostly, gore, sci-fi, monster, and bizarro short fiction.

She has also started work on her first full-length horror novel. She completed a BA Hons in Creative Writing and English Literature and has partaken in short courses and writers' groups since. In her spare time, she enjoys movies, bourbon, and heavy metal. Follow her at: facebook.com/AuthorMelanieWaghorne.

Jean Rabe has written thirty-three novels and more than seventy short stories in the military, urban fantasy, mystery, horror, western, and contemporary genres. Her latest novels are *Pockets of Darkness*, *The Love-Haight Case Files* (co-authored with Donald J. Bingle), and *The Cauldron* (co-authored with Gene DeWeese). She has also co-authored books with Andre Norton, F. Lee Bailey, and John Helfers, as well as written tie-in novels for Margaret Weis and Tracy Hickman's world of *Dragonlance*. You can find out more about her at: jeanrabe.com.

160

Acknowledgements

THIS PROJECT never would never have occurred but for the fact that magician and author William Pack wanted a compilation of ghost stories to accompany his presentations at libraries on familiar spirits and other ghostly encounters. You see, in addition to doing great magic acts for corporate events, Bill does storytelling presentations on such subjects as Houdini, Edgar Allen Poe, P.T. Barnum, The Great Chicago Fire, and, well, Familiar Spirits. Bill, a fine writer, himself, has authored books on the subject of each of his historical presentations, but had no volume on ghosts. I, in the meantime, had written a variety of books and stories—many of them dark or darkly humorous—and had critiqued and edited others in read and critique sessions at the GenCon Writers' Symposium and other forums and had been a participant in the St. Charles Writers' Group for more than fifteen years, but actually didn't have an anthology editing credit to my name. Then the chocolate fell into the peanut butter during a picnic in the graveyard and this anthology was born. Accordingly, my first thanks are to Bill for causing this to happen, as well as for creating the cover and cover design, formatting the book, and providing all sorts of advice and assistance on the project and the Kickstarter that funded and pre-marketed the book.

My next thanks go to the authors of the stories contained in *Familiar Spirits*: Sarah Hans, Dolores Whitt Becker, William Pack, Lynne Handy, Wren Roberts, Kate Johnson, Cathy Kern,

Ric Waters, TS Rhodes, Melanie Waghorne, and Jean Rabe. They wrote the stories, I merely edited them—yes, sometimes heavily, but sometimes hardly at all—and put them in a pleasing order, then set them free upon the world. If you like their stories in this volume, I encourage you to seek out these authors' other stories and books. Thanks, too, to Daniel ("Doc") Myers and Steven Saus, who wrote stories as stretch goal rewards, but whose stories did not end up in the book when fundraising failed to meet those goals.

Thanks to TS Rhodes, Danielle Ackley-McPhail, J.E. Mooney, Buck Hanno, Sarah Hans, and William Pack for offering rewards or stretch goal bonuses to help with the *Familiar Spirits* Kickstarter. Thanks, too, to all of my social media contacts on Twitter and Facebook and Goodreads, including friends, family, members of the St. Charles Writers' Group, the GenCon Writers' Symposium, and the Origins Game Fair Library, my fellow fans in the Supernatural, gaming, and writing communities, and past supporters of the Kickstarter for *Frame Shop* (a mystery thriller set in a suburban writers' group) for supporting this project not only with dollars, but with posts, shares, likes, tweets, and other boosts to visibility out there in the big wide world.

Thanks, also, to all of those who submitted stories for consideration for this anthology, but whose stories did not make the final cut. Many, many stories were excellent, but did not quite meet the tone and theme I was going for—an admittedly quite subjective criterion. Keep writing, keep trying, and pay close attention to the guidelines whenever and wherever you submit.

Finally, thanks to all of the Kickstarter backers, including:

_____; Danielle Ackley-McPhail; Adam T Alexander; Robin Allen; Mike Andreshak; Walt Anthony; Jessica B.; Christine Bell; Colleen Bell; Alistair Betts; Judy Betts; Richard Bingle; blank; Chad Bowden; Doug Burman; Kristi Cagle; Jerry Carden; Paul Cardullo; Tom & Linda Carey; Juan A Carrillo Jr.; Elaine M. Cassell; Stacy Chambers; Paul Chavez and Cate Pfeifer; Michael Cieslak; Colona Library; Jess Compton; Pam Crawford; Lark Cunningham; Amanda Curtis; Chris Davis; Deb; Leshia-Aimeé Doucet; Maxwell Alexander Drake; D-Rock; Robert Early; Fran Fredricks; Bram Prawira Gani; Anonymous Ghost; Michael Goldrich; Tina Noe Good; Joan E. Green; John Green; Lynne Handy; Róisín Harty; Mary Harville; Belinda Hatfield; Sheryl R. Hayes; John Herd; Paul Hill; Hubert Hobux; R. Holinger; Dorothy Holland; Theresa Hurley; Lisa Richelle Jensen; Amanda Johnson; H Lynnea Johnson; Tom Johnson; Ron Jolly; Mike Kenyon; Mary Konczyk; Kat Kremske; Laurna and Darcy; Randall Lemon; Lennhoff Family; Lester; Lizzy M.; Gail Z. Martin; Kevin Maxam; Doug McIntosh; Karen A Johnson Mead; S Mellor; Robert J. Mennella; Steven Mentzel; Gordon Meyer; Jeffrey Meyer; Donald Moore; Karen Mueller; Cyndi Myers, n/a; N/A; Ray Ninow; Mark Nocerino; Candi and Chris Norwood; John Patch; Angela Perry; Patrick & Sarah Pilgrim, Kevin Purtell; Chris Quinn; Jean Rabe; Ragnarok Publications; Lisa Ralph; Chris Bingle Redford; Rembert; Revek; Kathleen B. Roberts; Julie Robertson; RockPaperBooks.com; Roy Romasanta; Adriane Hughes Ruzak; Steven Saus; Jennifer Scepkowski; J.R. Schultz; Gregory B. Schwartz; Russell Smeaton; Ryan J. Smith; Tanya Spackman; Stephen D. Sullivan; Susan; Lori Linehan Swan; Steven C Swan; René

Tang; Simon Taylor; thatraja; Peter Thew; Mark and Leslie Thomas; Robby Thrasher; Joshua Tims; Elizabeth Vaughan; Gabrielle Vechmamontien; Stephanie Wagner; Markus Weber; Bill Weimer; Keith West; Tor André Wigmostad; Jamie Willman; and Martin Wilson.

I appreciate your support: past, present, and future. I hope you find this anthology darkly unsettling, but not so scary that you salt and burn it when you are finished.

Remember, an honest, thoughtful review is like treasure to independent authors and small press publishers. Conjuring up new readers can be more difficult than conjuring up *Familiar Spirits*.

Aloha.

Donald J. Bingle

September 2015

Books by William Pack

The Essential Houdini
The Essential P.T. Barnum
The Essential Great Chicago Fire
The Essential Edgar Allan Poe
The Essential Christmas Carol
Prairie Poets
Familiar Spirits

Available through williampack.com

"If you want to watch a group of adults mesmerized at an event, invite William. Three weeks later, those who attended still comment on the program. William captivated us with his stories. He brings energy, wit, and fascinating props and illustrations to a terrific program that will stay with you and your patrons. He engages the audience at every step of the program, entertains and educates with a twinkle in his eye."
-Elke Saylor, Muskego Library, WI

William is available for magical entertainment or educational programs custom suited for your event. For more information, please visit williampack.com

To contact William, email: bill@williampack.com

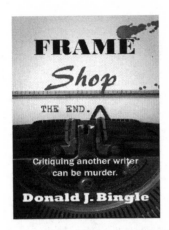

**Semi-Finalist in 2015
Soon-to-be-Famous
Illinois Author Competition**

From its lurid, over-the-top prologue to its quirky addendum, *Frame Shop* mixes violence, humor, and occasional writing advice in a format that will keep mystery lovers, aspiring authors, NaNoWriMo participants, and established writers turning the pages.

Harold J. Ackerman thinks his latest cat mystery proves he is the best writer in the Pleasant Meadows Writers' Guild and Critiquing Society, not that the motley assortment of poets, poseurs, and wannabe writers in the PMWGCS provides much competition. But then Gantry Ellis, the NYT best-selling author of the Danger McAdams mystery thrillers, joins the group and wows everyone. Still, Harold hopes to leverage his connection to the famous author into a big break, but soon his efforts lead to murder ... and then more murder.

Love-Haight is a comedy, locked within a mystery, hidden in a horror story... Wonderfully clever, stylish, and ghoulish. Delightfully twisted fun!
William C. Dietz
New York Times bestselling author

A seamless blend of horror, romance, and legal intrigue that makes for an urban fantasy-laced cocktail of literary delights sure to thrill readers of all stripes.
Matt Forbeck
New York Times bestselling author

Part fantasy noir, part supernatural legal thriller, Love-Haight sparkles with wit and originality.
Troy Denning
New York Times bestselling author

You have to enjoy a book where they kill the lawyer and he still defends his undead clients.
Jody Lynn Nye
New York Times bestselling author

Visit **donaldjbingle.com** for more information.